T0106533

LYING DOWN MOUNTAIN

THE
WHITE BUFFALO WOMAN TRILOGY

LYING DOWN MOUNTAIN

BOOK THREE

HEYOKA MERRIFIELD

ATRIA BOOKS
New York London Toronto Sydney

BEYOND WORDS
PUBLISHING

ATRIA BOOKS
A Division of Simon & Schuster, Inc.
1230 Avenue of the Americas
New York, NY 10020

BEYOND WORDS
PUBLISHING
20827 N.W. Cornell Road, Suite 500
Hillsboro, Oregon 97124-9808
503-531-8700 – 503-531-8773 fax
www.beyondword.com

Introductory quote on page ix, courtesy of John Kimmey, *Light on the Return Path* (Eugene, OR: Sacred Media, 1999)

The information contained in this book is intended to be educational. The author and publishers are in no way liable for any misuse of the information.

Managing editors: Henry Covi and Lindsay S. Brown
Proofreaders: Meadowlark Communications, Inc.
Cover design: Carol Sibley
Composition: William H. Brunson Typography Services
Interior artwork: Heyoka Merrifield
Cover artwork: Willow LaLand

First Atria Books/Beyond Words trade paperback edition July 2007

ATRIA BOOKS and colophon are trademarks of Simon & Schuster, Inc.

Beyond Words Publishing is a division of Simon & Schuster, Inc.

For more information about special discounts for bulk purchases, please contact Simon & Schuster Special Sales at 1-800-456-6798 or business@simonandschuster.com.

Manufactured in the United States of America

10 9 8 7 6 5 4 3 2 1

Library of Congress Cataloging-in-Publication Data

Merrifield, Heyoehkah
    Lying Down Mountain / Heyoka Merrifield.
        p. cm. — (White Buffalo Woman trilogy ; bk. 3)
        1. Indians of North America—Fiction. I. Title.
    PS3563.E7445L95   2007
    813'.54—dc22
                                2006100222

ISBN-13: 978-1-58270-153-0

The corporate mission of Beyond Words Publishing, Inc.: *Inspire to Integrity*

Dedication

For my medicine teachers, especially Grandfather
Tom Yellowtail, my spiritual father from the Crow
Tribe and my first Sundance chief. I honor all the
wisdom keepers who have been an inspiration to
me whether we walked through the Andes, the
Himalayas, or the mountains of Montana. All have
given me gifts that help me on my path of life. And
for the teachers who were always with me when
my heart was open enough to listen to them:
Mother Earth and Father Sky.

May the fragrance of love enter every human heart.

May that fragrance open our minds

to realize that we are all brothers and sisters.

May that realization inspire us to join hands and hearts

into a circle of love which can dream a new world into reality.

—David Monongye, Hopi Elder

Acknowledgments

My heartfelt gratitude goes out to all my friends who helped me by editing and typing my manuscript. I consider myself to be a storyteller and at the same time a somewhat challenged writer, but with their help, I am better at both. The following are a few members of my support group: Kelly Reed Morgen, Snow Deer, Karin Riley, Terrill Croghan, Harry Strunk, Janie Taylor, Christine White, Willow LaLand (cover design), Tim Houck (book design), and the entire staff at Beyond Words Publishing and Atria Books.

In celebration of
All My Relations

Chapter 1

The Jaguar

Twilight glowed above the faraway hills. The first birdsongs of morning began to celebrate the coming of the sun. Spotted Cat stood in silent meditation, facing the place of sunrise. Two eagles circling above the sleeping Earth were already touched by the sun. The Father of Light peeked over the distant horizon and Cat raised his arms in welcome to the new day. As the sun rose above the hills, a small breeze rippled across the land and danced through Spotted Cat's long black hair.

Cat started to sing the honoring song to the sun that Painted Story had taught him. The song spoke of the many gifts Father Sun gives to the Earth and all her children. He sang the song four times, then lowered his arms and let his gaze drift over the awakening hills.

Cat saw small dots of white moving across the hills and knew that antelope were starting to graze in the morning sun. He realized that by the time he walked to them the sun would be high over his head. As a hunter he had learned that, with their far superior vision, they could easily spot him standing on this hill, and if he walked toward them they would disappear like the wind. Trying not to look like a stalking hunter, he turned and walked away from them back down the hill until he came to a dry creek channel. Snaking along this low path, he made his way toward the antelope, crawling when necessary to keep hidden from their powerful eyesight.

When the sun was above Cat's head, he judged that the grazing antelope were close enough to hunt. Crouching behind a sagebrush, he strung his bow and drew out an arrow. He also removed two small plant skins from his pouch and tied them to the top branches of the bush. The tribe of the Peaceful People had gathered plant fibers and woven them into plant skins like the loincloth that Spotted Cat was wearing. This clothing was much more comfortable in this hot, dry climate than the animal skins worn by his tribe, the People of the Painted Earth Temple, who only wove baskets from the plant fibers.

The antelope stopped and stared at the small plant skins fluttering in the breeze atop the sagebrush. Cat had worked his way toward the antelope, staying downwind from them so the breeze would not betray his presence. The natural curiosity of the animals awoke, and one of them walked closer to have a better look. When it was within bow range, the antelope gave-away with one of Cat's arrows in its heart.

As he laid his hand on the animal to pray, Spotted Cat thought of Tree Spirit, his medicine teacher in the distant land of Gaia. The ceremony of thanking the antelope brought tears to his eyes as he remembered his beloved mentor. The strong, muscular animal, marked with white and tan, was a beautiful and sacred give-away.

He felt a presence standing near him and the hair on the back of his neck prickled. Spinning around, he could see nothing there. The still air came alive and encircled Cat. His hair and the feather he wore danced in the whirlwind. He realized that his thoughts of Tree Spirit had somehow called a part of his teacher to touch him. Cat sensed that his teachers in Gaia's Land would be pleased with his hunting ceremony.

Cat knew that when he ate the antelope its body would join with his body, bringing all the gifts

3

of its medicine powers. This animal was the swiftest in all the land and could run at top speed for a very long time. Cat felt honored that this gift would join with him and his adopted tribe.

Working swiftly, he sliced a long cut with his flint knife from the antelope's breastbone to its tail and removed the internal organs. Peeling back the hide by sliding the sharp knife close to its body, he carefully removed the skin. Once tanned, the soft antelope skin would become part of a comfortable winter shirt.

His preparation of the body finished, Spotted Cat placed the antelope's heart at the top of a nearby juniper tree as a gift to the eagles. He then wrapped the meat in the antelope's skin and tied the bundle to his back for the long walk back to the village. The trail took Cat through the Valley of Stories where the people often came for ceremony. Many paintings and carvings of the Peaceful People's stories decorated the canyon walls, and they reminded Spotted Cat of the paintings in the Cave Temple of his birth tribe. He sat down before a picture of a snake next to an Earth Mother symbol, the sacred spiral path of life.

The Peaceful People used tobacco as a sacred offering in their ceremonies and Cat took a handful from his pouch. He sprinkled tobacco on the Earth and placed into the ground a hawk feather he had found on his walk. He prayed for his lover, whom he had not seen for many years, and his tribe as they made their way on the long journey to Turtle Island. Spotted Cat felt good about his adopted tribe, though he longed to be with Calf, Grandmother Spider Woman, Tree Spirit, and the rest of his own people.

The Peaceful People reminded him in many ways of his tribe in Gaia's Land. This tribe walked the Sacred Balance Way more than any other he had contacted on the long journey to the heart of Turtle Island.

Cat's new teachers, Grandmother Crow and Grandfather Painted Story, radiated a similar powerful energy as Grandmother Spider Woman and Grandfather Tree Spirit. He hoped that his people's journey here would soon be over. Cat longed to be reunited with his tribe and the woman he loved, White Bison Calf. He imagined the People of the Painted Earth Temple sitting around the fire sharing stories with his newly adopted tribe.

The day was almost over when Spotted Cat saw the mountain that the Peaceful People's village was built upon. This new land had strange mountains with high, steep sides and large, flat tops. The people called this place the Land of the Lying Down Mountain.

The people built their lodges by sticking four rows of poles into the ground facing the four directions. They wove smaller poles into the large poles

eat the heart offering and then started flying north. He recognized the trail that he had taken when he journeyed to the Lying Down Mountain, and far away he saw a herd of buffalo walking south with a white buffalo as their leader. Suddenly, Cat realized that many hunters surrounded the herd. He screeched a warning in his eagle form, although he was not sure the buffalo could understand eagle talk. Instantly, the herd scattered as the hunters shot their arrows. The white buffalo broke through the circle of hunters and ran into the safety of a thick forest.

Cat awoke drenched in sweat with his heart pounding. After calming himself with the morning sun ceremony, he returned to Painted Story's lodge and told his medicine teacher about the dream. The elder sat for a while in deep thought with his eyes closed before he responded.

"Jaguar, sometimes we can see the actual waking world in our dreams, although more often dreams speak to us with symbols. You can best interpret your own dream symbols because they are from a very deep part of yourself. I sense that the one you love is on her journey south and you will soon be reunited."

The spotted cat that walked in Cat's new homeland was much larger than the snow leopard of the land of his birth. Like the medicine teachers from Gaia's Land, Painted Story recognized that Cat's power animal helper and namesake was the spotted cat. Now known by his tribe as Jaguar, Spotted Cat felt good about having a new name to celebrate being in a new land.

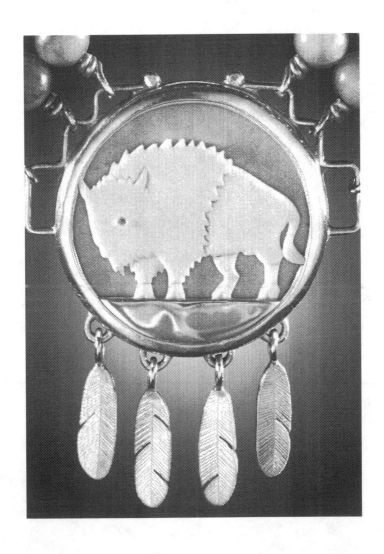

Chapter 2

The White Buffalo

The white buffalo led her herd into a lush meadow surrounded by a dense forest. The grass was a young, tender new growth after a late-autumn rainy season. Deep in the Earth, she could smell the passing of her buffalo tribe earlier in the year. They had stayed long and grazed the grass away, leaving dark brown soil as they migrated north. Within the wisdom of her body, she could feel the migrations of her tribe's many generations that had stopped to eat in this place. The new grasses grew sweet and fragrant, and the white grandmother buffalo's mind drifted to the needs of her herd.

There was a new grandfather buffalo now that the old grandfather was wounded and lame. The old warrior had been gored in the shoulder during a battle for supremacy and was not healing well. He lagged behind whenever the herd was on the move. Recently, a small pack of wolves had attacked him and a few calves that walked with him. She had been able to run back and guide the herd to quickly surround the young calves in a protective circle. Faced with a ring of horns, the wolves had given up their hunt, but she realized that it was just a matter of time before the old grandfather would give-away to predators. He grazed close by her now, favoring his stiff, swollen leg.

The white leader of the buffalo tribe closed her eyes in the sunlight. She felt great joy in leading this strong herd through lush grasslands. But hidden deep in her body's mind, a forgotten thought tugged at her. There seemed to be something she meant to do on this migration, and another tribe that could benefit from her wisdom. A distant memory awoke in the white buffalo; she held the Web of Life teachings to gift to the people of this land.

A loud cry brought the grandmother buffalo out of her deep meditations. Above her an eagle screeched loudly, and in her nose a scent screamed an even louder alarm. Humans!

She bellowed to the herd to flee south, reaching out to the group mind to turn in that direction. The old grandfather buffalo fell at her side with three arrows in his heart. Other arrows flew in the air and several hunters ran toward him with clubs to make a quick death of her old companion. The herd fled in all directions and thundered away, leaving her alone as she ran south.

The white buffalo ran until she was winded, then slowed to a walk to catch her breath. She came to a stream and stood still, turning her ears to the north. There was no sound of pursuit, so she tasted the gentle northerly breeze with her nose until she was content that no hunters were near.

The tired buffalo bent down and took a long cool drink. Her legs trembled with fatigue as she lay down to rest. She set all her senses on guard in case any predators approached and then drifted into the dream world. *She was with Grandmother Spider Woman in the Painted Earth Temple. Spider Woman was explaining to her that, as a young priestess, she must learn about the Web of Life so she could pass the teachings on to future generations.*

She awoke suddenly from her dream to the scent of humans. A circle of hunters surrounded her, though their bows were not drawn. They looked tired from being loaded down with the large bundles of buffalo meat tied to their backs.

The hunters stared in amazement at the beautiful woman in a decorated fringed white buckskin dress. Having followed the footprints of a buffalo

13

to this spot, they realized that the white buffalo woman asleep by the stream was a medicine woman or perhaps a sorceress.

White Buffalo Woman sat up and smiled at the hunters, as her mind flooded with the long-forgotten memories of her time as a priestess in Gaia's Land. "Have no fear," she signed with her hands. "I have brought you a medicine gift from a far distant land. Take me to your village and we can celebrate this gift together."

One of the women hunters came up to White Buffalo, gave her a warm hug, and signed, "I am called Morning Star and you are welcome to stay in my lodge." Although the priestess from Gaia's Land still hurt from the loss of her herd, she was happy to be back in human form and knew that the hunters had simply been following the natural order of life. So when the tribe invited her to walk south with them toward their village, she gladly followed.

As they drew near the circle of Earth-covered lodges, White Buffalo saw many plants growing close together and surrounding the village. She had never seen this kind of plant before and asked Morning Star about it.

"We call this plant corn and it is very important to my tribe, the Friendly People. Long ago, as our ancestors traveled in a land far away in the south, they gathered this plant's grain. It became their primary food and they learned to grind the dried seeds between stones to make a white powder. They mixed this ground cornmeal with water and baked it on a hot hearthstone.

The ancient Grandmother Priestess of our tribe had a medicine dream one night. A goddess came to her dressed in green like the leaves of the corn plant. Her hair was the color of the tops of the corn, and she held a bundle of cornstalks with much larger ears than the variety that the people gathered in the wild. She gave our priestess a ceremony to honor the corn plant during the autumn equinox. We were to save the largest, most perfect ears of grain each year and use them to perform a ceremony of honoring and thankfulness.

The seeds from this bundle were to be like children to the tribe. At the time of the winter solstice, we used the basket of corn seed as part of the Longest Night ceremony. In the time of spring equinox, these seeds were to be put back into our Mother Earth and she would give birth to more corn plants. The Corn Goddess told our Grandmother to talk to our children seeds, encouraging them to grow strong and tall. She told them to be loving and respectful to the growing Corn Maiden stalks, telling them that we would take care of their most perfect children and return them to Mother Earth. We were to be good nursemaids to the Corn Maidens and they would become like members of our tribe. Over many, many winters, the ears of corn grew much larger and they became the most sacred food of the Friendly People."

After White Buffalo Woman settled into Morning Star's lodge, she asked to use Star's carving tools. Buffalo wanted to craft two pipes to be used in a give-away ceremony. The Powers had helped her envision a ceremony that would be called "the Making of Relations." Star gifted her with two types of stone, one red and one black, which her tribe used in the making of their pipes. With the red stone she made a pipe for herself and with the black stone she carved a pipe for the Friendly People. On her new pipe bowl she carved a buffalo and on the black pipe she sculpted a spider.

White Buffalo Woman asked Morning Star to take part in the new ceremony and to invite six more elders. The eight medicine people sat around the central fire, watched over by the stars of the night sky. The rest of the tribe sat surrounding the medicine circle as Buffalo started the ceremony.

"Tribe of the Friendly People, I bring a gift from Gaia's Land to you. The teachings I am giving to you are from my Grandmother Priestess. As I have journeyed over the past winters to your land, my trail has been long and difficult. In the land of my birth, there was much killing, and my tribe attempted to journey here together, though almost all of them perished in the wars.

You have been so kind to me that I feel I again have a family. Morning Star has become my sister and her parents are now my mother and father. You are all related to me, and now I would like to honor our new family with a ceremony."

Morning Star had decorated a pipe bag with quills in the pattern of a spider's web. From this bag, Buffalo took the black pipe carved with a spider on it.

"In this medicine pipe I placed all the love, kindness, and goodness that I feel in your circle. It is black to honor the Mother of Creation: the 'Sacred Void.' The carved

17

spider on the pipe is to celebrate the powers of the Web of Life, the teaching I bring from Gaia's Land. And in this ceremony, I say to all the Powers that you and I have now become relations.

As I traveled across the top of our Mother Earth, many tribes aided me and became my friends. Their kindness helped me see the deep wisdom in the stories of the Web of Life and the Sacred Balance. In the beginning of creation, the First Human Mother wove the Web of Life by weaving two luminous strands of energy to connect the Four Sacred Powers, forming a cross. Radiating in strands from the center of this cross were woven all the families of creatures. Finally, First Mother wove a spiral web onto this medicine circle, and wherever the strands touched, a being's spirit lived. Some were plant beings, some were human beings, some were stone beings, and so on for every being in the All That Is. With this touching, the luminous Web of Life connected all the many parts of Mother Earth and Father Sky.

This is why it is possible to feel connected to all of Creation. When we forget that we are all connected and that what we do affects the entire web, we lose sight of our place within the Sacred Balance. In the land of my birth, the Sacred Balance Way is more and more forgotten, but in this land of Turtle Island, I feel that the Sacred Balance Way of my ancestors will live on for a long Age.

The Medicine Pipe that holds this ceremony of Making of Relations will help you and your children's children remember that all parts of Creation are connected. Notice that often when people smoke their pipes, they become quiet and inwardly peaceful. When you use your pipes in this ceremonial medicine way, you may go deeper into this meditative place.

Before you smoke, join the pipe bowl and stem together and say, 'In celebration of All My Relations.' As you perform this joining, envision the coming together of the sacred twins of creation: the Earth Mother and the Sky Father. As you put tobacco into the pipe, call in the many powers of the Universe. When fire joins with the tobacco, the smoke will make your breath visible. This will help you envision your prayers traveling and touching every part of the Web of Life and keep you connected with all of Creation.

After I smoke the sacred pipe, she will be passed around the circle so each person can send their prayers into the All That Is. You may ask for healing and for finding the path toward giving your personal gifts of power to the Web of Life."

White Buffalo Woman raised the pipe bowl and the stem in her hands and in deep meditation joined them together, saying, "In celebration of All My Relations." With each pinch of tobacco she added to the pipe, she invited another power into it. She called the Earth Mother, the Great Spirit, and the Powers of the Four Directions. Next she honored the plants, animals, and ancestors. White Buffalo Woman then offered the pipe stem to the Earth, the sky, and the four directions before she put a coal of fire on the tobacco and smoked. She prayed for her new relatives in this circle and for her relatives in the Spirit World. She sent her prayers of protection to her beloved Spotted Cat.

She then passed the pipe sun-wise around the circle and each medicine person sent prayers to the Universe with the smoke. After they were finished, she sent her voice with the smoke again. She separated the pipe and stem, saying, "In celebration of all the People."

White Buffalo returned the pipe to its bag and handed it to Morning Star before speaking again.

"Morning Star will be the keeper of the sacred pipe, and she will bring it to your future ceremonies. Also, you may wish to make a ceremonial pipe to use in your own personal meditations. The stones and decorations you use can be personal and sacred to you.

In the friendly manner that comes so naturally to this tribe, you may also make relatives of other tribes you come in contact with. This can help end any hostilities or wars in this land. You can encourage the young men to compete in games instead of war. If the people play at races, wrestling, and spear-throwing, it will help to keep death and hatred from poisoning your contact with other tribes. The games can be designed to bring a closer relationship instead of a separation. In this way the Sacred Balance can be experienced, and everyone will know that they are connected in the Web of Life. The Sacred Pipe Ceremony and the Making of Relations Ceremony will help to bring peace to this rich, abundant land."

Chapter 3

The Sacred Twins

White Buffalo Woman stayed for a while with her new family. They talked about the lands to the south and the place of the Lying Down Mountain. The Friendly People described the trails she must travel to arrive at the village of one of their tribe's clans, the Peaceful People.

One morning, Buffalo knew it was time to leave and continue her journey. She took Morning Star in her arms and started to cry.

"Star, you have been a sister to me and I do not want to be separated from you. These years of travel have been exhausting, frightening, and lonely.

Other people have befriended and helped me. I have met wonderful, wise teachers and seen beautiful, strange lands. The Web of Life teachings that the High Priestess entrusted me to bring to your land have helped me stay focused. The great responsibility of keeping so many ages of priestesses' wisdom has made me brave and helped me overcome difficulties. Also, the knowledge that I will be rejoined with my sacred twin partner has kept me on the path of this long journey.

My spiritual brother and the one I love, Spotted Cat, is traveling before me, and I feel that he will be found in the land of the Peaceful People. Eyes of Wisdom, a wise woman in a tribe to the north, met with him as he passed south through her village. She sent him to the Land of the Lying Down Mountain to study with the one who taught her.

Grandmother Spider Woman, who was our High Priestess in Gaia's Land, trained both Spotted Cat and myself to become the Shaman and Priestess of our people. We started our apprenticeship at a young age and were very close during our childhood.

We lived in a beautiful valley beneath the snow-capped White Mountain. Our village was happy and peaceful and our temple was in a great cave painted with many medicine animals. The Painted Temple was very famous and other tribal people traveled long distances for ceremonies held there.

As we got older, the friendship that Cat and I shared grew to a deep love. When the warring tribes began to attack our people, Cat left to scout a safe passage to your island for our tribe.

We have been separated for so many winters that I fear he has forgotten me. We have both gone through so many changes. Will we still be able to relate in a beautiful way? Do you think Cat will be displeased with the things I have chosen to do on the journey from Gaia's Land to Turtle Island?"

Morning Star hugged her tightly. "Do not worry, my friend. I am sure your meeting with Spotted Cat will go well, for your heart is in a good place. You have become a wise teacher, and the difficulties and challenges of your journey have given you strength and wisdom. I am sure Spotted Cat will be understanding of the directions your life has taken you in the past winters."

That night, the tribe held a huge feast to honor White Buffalo Woman. They sang many songs and the drumming continued far into the night. As Buffalo lay down to rest, the songs still echoed in the darkness, helping her to drift into a peaceful sleep.

In the dream world, White Buffalo Woman was flying south, beating her crow wings in the night air. Dawn was breaking over the horizon as she flew over flat, dry earth. Suddenly, the ground opened beneath her to reveal a huge, dark canyon. The cold morning wind swirled up through the great abyss, throwing her to and fro while she struggled to fly south. As the sun began to illuminate the canyon, it glowed as if painted gold, red, and purple.

Flying past the Painted Canyon, she looked down on a village where many people were dancing in ceremony. She descended and landed on the head of a kachina dancer. Her wings became part of the dancer's mask as her crow spirit moved within the dancer.

White Buffalo Woman awoke from this dream wrapped in a feeling of warmth and well-being. She had packed her travel bundle before the feast so she could leave the village with the first light of day. Morning Star and several other hunters accompanied her for the first days of her journey and hunted elk on the southern trail.

As White Buffalo Woman began her journey south, Jaguar was feeling restless. He had been so ever since his dream of the white buffalo, and he finally decided to make a good store of meat for the coming winter in order to distract himself. For him, the strongest medicine animal he hunted in this new land was the Elk Tribe. The elk were strong, magical animals with incredible endurance. If an elk scented the hunter before he came near enough for a shot, he would not see it again. Jaguar had tracked these animals for days without getting close. Often, the tracks would circle around, and he could see where the elk had stood behind a tree and watched him as he carefully examined the prints on the ground.

The late fall was mating season for the Elk Tribe. While the males challenged each other for supremacy of the herd, they dropped their normal caution and became easier to hunt. Jaguar liked to hunt at the higher elevations to the north where the grass was still green. He would walk through the forest until he found footprints or other signs, like the wallows they made in areas where a spring came out of the Earth. There, the elk would dig out a pit large enough to lie in so they could bathe during the heat of midday.

As Jaguar walked along a north-facing slope, he caught the scent of elk and came upon a trail that led down to a wallow with many recently made footprints. Finding a hiding place behind a tree above the wallow, Jaguar strung his bow and took out an arrow. He pulled up a blade of grass, held it between his two thumbs, and blew on it. The shrill sound imitated the call of a female elk. Soon Jaguar heard the brush snapping and knew that a lone male elk was coming to find a mate.

Jaguar bent his bow as the elk came into view and waited until its head was behind a tree with its body still in sight. The swift, unseen arrow found the elk's heart and the animal fled, crashing noisily through the brush.

Jaguar paused for a moment before stepping out from behind the tree. Experience had taught him that running after the elk would give it a burst of energy from the pursuit, and it would run a very long distance. If he simply sat quietly for a moment, the elk would go a short distance, then lie down to rest while its life force drained into the Earth. Soon, the elk would not have the strength to get up and its spirit would drift into the Spirit World. While he waited, Jaguar sat and ate his midday meal of dried antelope meat and gave thanks for the elk's give-away.

Jaguar was several days north of the village, so his plan was to cut the meat into small strips and dry them. This would take a few days and he decided to camp in this place for a while. Following the trail left by the wounded elk, Jaguar found the still animal and reached into his bundle to take out his flint knife and tobacco pouch. As he reached into the pouch for an offering, the knife slipped out of his grip. Once while hunting, he had broken his flint knife and it had been extremely difficult to carve the deer he had felled with only the broken flint shards. As he quickly stooped to grab the knife, an arrow whistled over his head and stood quivering in the trunk of a nearby tree.

Jaguar jumped for cover in the brush, grabbing his bow while in the air, and ran as fast as his legs would carry him. Without looking behind him, he sprinted to the top of the next hill. As he ran over the crest, he threw himself down on the ground panting and peeked back toward the elk. A large group of hunters surrounded the animal and one was holding up Jaguar's knife and hollering. The others were laughing and shoving each other and chattering in a strange tongue. He sensed that they were making fun of his fright as he ran away, but soon they became more interested in the meat and started to carve up the elk.

The men looked hungry, and Jaguar felt that their interest in the meat had replaced their interest in him. He turned south and headed toward the safety of his village. In all his time on Turtle Island, he had not encountered any tribes that were hostile or whose people considered those outside their tribe to be enemies. The land was so abundant with food that he could not understand why anyone would attack him.

Jaguar also worried for the village of the Peaceful People. They must be warned that these Nomadics were hunting not far from the village. He feared that this new Wild Tribe might want to attack the village to steal corn, now that the crops had been harvested. As Jaguar journeyed nearer and nearer to his village, lost in his thoughts, he had little idea that White Buffalo Woman also traveled the same trails a short distance away.

Her back bundle was full of dried elk meat as she walked south alone. The country became more and more dry as she traveled. The trees grew smaller there, and Buffalo walked whole days among hills that hardly had any trees. As the land became more desertlike, the many-colored crimson canyons and rock formations took her breath away.

The Friendly People had talked about the Red Rock Land and she knew to drink lightly from her waterskins. Sometimes many miles stretched between places where water flowed. In one of the red canyons, she found a little stream that flowed over the edge into a clear pool. It was a lovely spot, and White Buffalo decided to camp for a while and replenish her food by hunting the numerous rabbits with her sling. The pool she found at the base of the stream rejuvenated her sore body, especially her feet.

In the morning after a pleasant night's rest, Buffalo packed her bundle. As she started to pour water on her campfire, she was suddenly grabbed forcefully from behind. The attacker pushed her down, tearing her buckskin dress, and she struck the ground with her back, knocking the breath from her lungs. As she gasped for air, she could see several other men, laughing and yelling war cries.

When the man who had pushed her down jumped on top of her, Buffalo lifted her arms behind her head and grabbed a fist-sized rock. With both hands, she struck the top of his head with such force that he collapsed unconscious to the ground. Seizing another rock, she threw it at the man who had led the war cries. It struck him in the mouth, and teeth and blood sprayed over the red ground.

During the confusion caused by her attack, White Buffalo picked up her bundle and ran down the canyon. Behind her, the fallen leader screamed and held his jaw while blood trickled down his cheek. When Buffalo's rock had smashed his mouth, his teeth had snapped down in surprise and bitten off the tip of his tongue. The four other men reached out to help him, but he pushed them away, instead shouting incoherently and pointing toward the fleeing woman. The four took off in pursuit while he splashed water on his face and held his aching mouth. The other fallen man lay still on the Earth.

Not far from where Buffalo fled through the silent canyons of the Red Rock Land, Jaguar also walked over the crimson ground. He chose his path carefully, worried that he might encounter more of the Nomadics. When he discovered the footprints of six people in the chalky dust of the road, he decided to climb to the top of the canyon, where he could move along the rim and see them below. Moving silently, he soon overtook six men carrying hunting weapons. From the way they were dressed, the men looked like they were from the same tribe that had attacked him.

Jaguar followed their movements for some time until, to his horror, the band attacked a woman camped by a small waterfall. The woman fought back bravely and wounded two of them, then ran down the canyon. Anxious to help her, Jaguar cut across a bend in the canyon and stood ready to ambush the four men as they came around the corner. The first one fell with an arrow in his chest. The second arrow missed the chest of another pursuer, wounding him in the leg. Jaguar aimed at another running man but missed him altogether, instead striking the neck of the already wounded man and killing him swiftly. With two men dead, the remaining two quickly retreated back up the canyon trail.

Jaguar cut across another large loop in the canyon and scrambled down the side to the bottom. White Buffalo had left her bow at the waterfall and was now pulling out her sling from her bundle. Seeing that she could run no further, she dodged behind a large boulder to attack her pursuers.

As she stood panting and peeking around the boulder, she heard a sudden movement behind her. She spun around, blindly launching a hissing rock in the air toward her stunned enemy's head . . . who she suddenly realized had his hands outward in a sign of peace. The poor man ducked and the singing rock grazed his ear, just missing his head. Horrified by her mistake, Buffalo ran toward him to help, but seeing her rapid approach, the man howled and desperately searched for somewhere to hide.

"Spotted Cat!" White Buffalo gasped, stopped in her tracks by the shock of recognition. She ran and threw her arms around the confused Jaguar. The stinging in his ear faded away as he finally recognized his loved one. In the midst of their embrace, White Buffalo Woman remembered that she was being pursued and they were still in danger. "Cat, we must flee. Several men attacked me a little while ago. Some of them are chasing me and may soon be here."

Jaguar smiled and touched her face, feeling like he was in a dream. "From the top of the canyon, Calf,

I saw two of the men defeated by a strong warrioress. Two more now lie dead from my arrows in the canyon. The remaining two are now running north, away from us. Still, we should be careful while we remain in the Red Rock Land. Walk south with me toward my adopted tribe, the Peaceful People. We can talk and put as much distance between these violent people and ourselves as we can today. Why are you alone? Where are Grandmother Spider Woman, Tree Spirit, and all the others?"

As they walked together holding hands, tears streamed down White Buffalo Woman's face.

"Almost all of our tribe is in the World of Spirit. After Cricket arrived back home, we met to discuss our journey to Turtle Island. As we talked, the Slave Tribe attacked and killed most of the People of the Painted Earth Temple. Luckily, Spider Woman, Tree Spirit, and I were underground in the Cave Temple and survived the attack. Sadly, Blue Bird, Little Fox, Shy Dove, and Star Raven were the only others to survive. All four were wounded and decided to stay in Gaia's Land with Star Raven's tribe.

Grandmother felt she would not survive the long journey and decided to remain alone in the Painted Earth Temple. While she performed her ceremony of leaving her body, Tree Spirit and I closed the door of the temple with an avalanche of rocks.

We traveled together as far as the land of the Tribes of the White Reindeer. On the edge of their land, a Slave Tribe attacked and took me prisoner. Tree Spirit sneaked back and freed me from my bonds, then climbed high above the Tribe on a cliff. From there, he attacked my captors with his bow so I could escape. Many of the warrior people died before they were able to slay Tree Spirit."

Now tears fell from Jaguar's eyes as well while the two walked. With their arms around each other's waists, their tears fell onto the trail that was leading them to their new life.

That night, White Buffalo Woman sat leaning against Jaguar as his arms encircled her. They stared into the campfire and thought about their life together in Gaia's Land. There was much to say, although their embrace itself was like a deep conversation. Buffalo finally broke the silence. "Cat, I want to say so much, but I do not know how to begin." Taking a deep breath, she plunged into her story.

"During my stay with the People of the White Reindeer, I became the apprentice to a great medicine man. His name was Drumming Deer and he was away when you visited the tribe. This shaman taught me how to travel into other worlds that exist at the same time as the world we walk in now. The first time I was able to travel this way, a crow became my helper. I wanted to see you, and in the crow's body I flew to a Cavelike-Temple-House where you sat in ceremony. The people around you wore medicine animal masks."

Jaguar sat up straight and spoke excitedly.

"I remember that ceremony. We performed it in a kiva, the Peaceful People's name for their temples. It means world below. The kivas are built like their Earth-covered homes, except the door is in the middle of the roof. We enter into the kiva by a ladder, which makes the dwelling feel more like a cave. The walls are painted like our cave temples and, like our temples, it feels as though we have entered into the womb of our Mother Earth.

When the crow flew into the kiva, I thought of you and knew that you were safe. But when the crow seemed to fade away into the air, some of the villagers were afraid. They argued over whether this was a medicine sign or a visit from a sorcerer. I said the crow made me feel good and most of the people agreed.

They decided the visit was a good sign for our ceremony because the Crow Mother Dancer is called the Mother of All Kachinas. Kachina is their name for the Powers in the Spirit World. Crow Mother is always present during our initiation ceremonies."

Buffalo smiled at the memory and continued her story. "While in the land of the People of the North Star, I entered into the other world by accident. There, a young man named Sun Eagle desired me for his mate. When I fell into this other world, it seemed good to fulfill his desire. Together, we had children, and he grew old and died while I stayed the same age. At the ceremony of his death, I remembered you. My memories of this world rushed back to me, and I felt as though only an instant had passed. It was as if one thought had become a whole life, which now seems only a dream. I am so sorry, Cat. I did not mean to betray you."

Jaguar stiffened and sat frowning into the fire. Buffalo felt a wall begin to grow between the man she loved and herself. Jaguar sat silent for a long time before he spoke. "I feel my stomach has disappeared and I am falling into the black void where it used to be. I remember Eagle from my stay in his village. He was not my favorite person, though I felt close to his brother, Owl." Jaguar paused for a moment before continuing.

"Calf, I also fear to tell you something I did during our separation. Among the Peaceful People there is a girl named Hummingbird. She was very kind to me and we became friends. She wanted to become my mate until I told her about you. She understood that I was promised to another, though it made her sad. One night after the ceremony to bless the corn seeds planted in Mother Earth, we went for a walk. The full moon smiled down on us and we were swept away in a moment of passion. Afterward, I felt very confused, for she is a kind, gentle person and I did not want to cause her any pain. But Calf, I know my heart is joined with yours."

Now it was White Buffalo Woman's turn to stare silently into the fire for a while. "I suddenly understand the dizzy feelings in your stomach. We both have been through many challenges the past few winters, and this seems to me to be the greatest challenge of all. But we have survived so many dangers to be reunited, it would be sad to let these events come between us."

With a deep breath they both relaxed, and White Buffalo felt the wall between them dissolve away. "Our hearts have drawn us back together from one side of Mother Earth to the other side. I feel like she has blessed our union. We were born to be Sacred Twins like the Mother and Father of Creation, and I feel not even death could separate us now." White Buffalo Woman and Jaguar embraced in love medicine until they fell asleep in each other's arms by the fire. After a while, the fire also went to sleep.

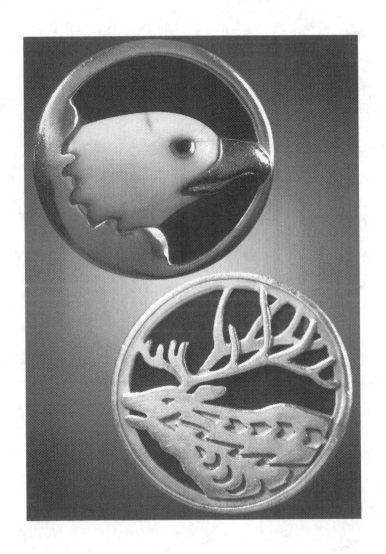

Chapter 4

The Lying Down Mountain

The moon had gone from her full face to the time of new birth when White Buffalo and Jaguar at last saw the Lying Down Mountain in the distance. The expansive land stretched before them in all directions to a far horizon. A huge Thunder Cloud gave his blessings to the Earth as he danced through the blue sky far to the west. Although this place was dry, it seemed peaceful and inviting. Buffalo felt a deep sense of goodness at the first view of her new home when a rainbow appeared over the flat-topped mountain.

The sky seemed vast and far away. More thunderclouds rose to the heavens. She remembered her dreams as a crow and already felt familiar with the Peaceful People's village. White Buffalo Woman knew that she would soon be a part of the Peaceful People's ceremonies in the cave kivas. The thought of being a part of a tribal people who were at peace with each other and the Earth thrilled her. Buffalo's heart filled with joy as they walked toward the Lying Down Mountain.

The Peaceful People saw them coming from a long distance and the village stirred with excitement. Jaguar was the best hunter in the village and there was usually a feast when he returned from a hunt. Elk was the favorite meal of many of the villagers and most of them stood outside their lodges now, ready to welcome the travelers.

Painted Story and Grandmother Crow were at the front of the crowd when Buffalo and Jaguar arrived at the village center. Grandmother Crow smiled. "It is said that whenever the great Jaguar goes hunting, he never comes back empty-handed. And although you do not have a huge bundle of elk meat, I see that you are not empty-handed." The People laughed and some of them patted Jaguar on the back. "Who is this wonderful woman who shines with an inner light like a wise grandmother?"

Jaguar took Buffalo's hand and placed it in Grandmother Crow's. "This is White Bison Calf, the same woman who appears in the stories I have told about my life in Gaia's land. In this land she has become White Buffalo Woman. She is the Priestess of the People of the Painted Earth Temple, though that tribe now numbers only two people."

Painted Story took Buffalo's other hand. "Seeing the glow that comes from both of you, I foretell that your tribe will increase in numbers soon." With another roar of laughter, the people took turns greeting White Buffalo, telling her their names and their relationships to all the many gathered villagers. She was soon lost in the great web of names and relations—who was whose aunt or second cousin. Finally, Grandmother rescued the new visitor by inviting her and Jaguar for a meal in the lodge she shared with Painted Story.

While they ate, White Buffalo Woman talked much about her journey from Gaia's Land. She shared the news from Gaia and the different tribes she had encountered on her long journey. Painted Story was very interested and asked many questions. She finished her story by telling them of the Nomadic Tribe's attack only half a moon's walk to the north.

Jaguar, who had been sitting thoughtfully silent, spoke up as her story ended. "We need to prepare the village in case of attack. The Nomadics may try to raid the village to steal corn for the coming winter. We must organize the hunters to also become scouts. If we each take a different direction in our hunting, the Wild Tribe will not come into our land unnoticed. Also, we must take turns being out at night so attackers will not surprise us during the dark hours. We can pile stones to be used as weapons at the tops of the cliff trails leading to our village. We must create a signal known by all the tribe so we can gather quickly for defense."

Grandmother Crow looked concerned.

"I see that you have given much thought to this defense, Jaguar. After hearing White Buffalo's stories of the warring tribes in Gaia's Land, I can see more fully the wisdom of our ancestors. We too migrated from Gaia's Land long, long ago, after the cataclysmic Earth changes. We journeyed by way of the Great Water in boats made of reeds, sailing from one stepping-stone island to another.

The Tribe of the Peaceful People has often been gifted with medicine people who were seers. Sometimes they were able to see far into the future. They predicted the change in Gaia's Land as her tribes became more and more warlike. That is why we chose to come to Turtle Island.

44

During the time of the Earth-shaking, the islands bumped together and some even disappeared. The powerful island of Aztlán was lost when it sank into the water. These great changes in the Earth wiped out whole tribes of animals and peoples, but Turtle Island held her arms open to the displaced peoples from Gaia.

It has been peaceful here since that time, with very little war between the peoples of this land. Our tribe has never been warlike, although we can easily defend ourselves from the slopes of the Lying Down Mountain.

You may organize the hunters as you see fit, Jaguar. You have more experience with warring tribes and you will make a good leader if an attack occurs. But as the spiritual leaders of the tribe, Painted Story or I may have another plan for the defense of our village.

Our relationship with the Kachinas of Rain has been very close and loving this year. After every ceremony in which we have asked for their help, they have come. Every time our corn was dry, they came to bless it with rain. This corn harvest has become the most abundant in any of our elders' memories. We have twice the amount of food stored away that we need to feast well throughout the next cycle of seasons.

Be careful with your defense plans and leave room for another way of preventing an attack. Our minds are powerful and can sometimes create events that are not always for our higher good. Along with your preparation for a violent defense, keep a peaceful way of seeing a possible future."

Painted Story spoke after Grandmother Crow:

"Jaguar, instead of throwing large rocks and arrows down on our wandering neighbors, let us instead invite them to White Buffalo Woman's ceremony of Making of Relations. We can offer them half of our abundant harvest so they will be well fed in the coming winter. We can also teach them how to grow corn and have relationships with both the Corn Maidens and the Kachinas of Rain. Without this knowledge, it would do them very little good to put seeds into this dry Earth.

White Buffalo Woman arrived in our land at the same time as the Nomadic Tribes.

I feel that her coming is a sign from the Sacred Powers: we have always attempted to take the peaceful way and we must stay true to our tribe's sacred path."

Jaguar smiled at Painted Story and Grandmother Crow. "As always, your wisdom is a guidance at every fork in the path we all must walk. The Making of Relations ceremony will be the path that is in my heart. I will only walk the path of defense if the way of peace is not accepted."

White Buffalo Woman was pleased. This small council had reflected a medicine wisdom that was close to her heart, but she was still troubled. "Grandparents, how did the Earth become so imbalanced that she destroyed many people, animals, and whole islands?"

Painted Story sighed.

"This is too large a question for a small answer, my granddaughter. The stories passed down from our ancestors say that such Earth-changes have occurred three times. They say that we exist now in the Fourth World, after each of the first three worlds was destroyed at the end of its Great Age.

It was the People of Aztlán who held most of the responsibility for the ending of the last world. They lived on an island in the Great Sea toward the place of sunrise, creating amazing tools and even stranger stories. These island people were able to carve and move huge stones to build their lodges and temples, some crafted like huge pointed mountains. They also created long, hollow lodges like reeds that were large enough for many people to sit inside. The Aztláns could make these lodges fly through the air and travel long distances in a short time, by capturing the life force from the All That Is.

Soon, they began to feel superior to all the other humans on Mother Earth. They visited other tribes for pure amusement, viewing them as primitive creatures. These feelings of superiority caused them to lose contact with the Sacred Balance, as they began to expand and build their villages in other peoples' lands. Whenever they built their villages, they tried to control the tribes nearby. The Aztláns viewed these people as babies in need of their teachings and began to force them to serve as slaves, to sew clothes and grow food.

Within their lives of comfort and plenty, the People of Aztlán became restless. They began to harness the power of All That Is to deform the slave tribes into more entertaining creatures, combining animals with the human slaves. These part-humans, part-animals were to the Aztláns what toys are to our children, and the Aztláns became more and more arrogant with every creation.

The delicate balance that holds all life together on Mother Earth was affected by this unnatural control. A tear ripped through the fabric that holds Mother Earth and Father Sky in balance, causing changes in the weather and shakings in the Earth. All tribes suffered from the destructive changes, and even the path that Mother Earth travels through Father Sky was altered. On this new path, Mother Earth passed close by a star in the sky. Their meeting caused huge destruction throughout all the Earth, and so it was that the Third Age came to an end.

Whole islands were destroyed. Many people were killed or displaced. The survivors had to live in caves or underground villages to escape the massive destruction on the surface. The Peaceful People were one of the tribes, hiding underground for a long time.

I believe that the warring tribes in Gaia's Land, the ones you call the Slave Tribes, are the descendants of the People of Aztlán. For too long, they have felt superior to the people who live close to the natural balance with the Earth and her creatures. If they continue making war and become masters of all the tribes of Earth, the Fourth Age will also come to an end. The survival of all humans depends on tribes like ours that continue to walk the way of the Sacred Balance.

We are one of the keepers of the way that can make the Fourth Age a time of peace and abundance. With our ceremonies and vision, we can create a balanced relationship with all of life. As long as the Peaceful People and other tribes with similar intent keep true to this path, the Fourth Age will not end in another cataclysm.

Like your tribe, the People of the Painted Earth Temple, we have always strived to walk the Earth within the Sacred Balance. We honor and interact with all life and know that what happens to one part of

life affects us all. Whether in our ceremonies or our daily work, we know that
what we do causes balance or imbalance in
our interdependent relationship with the All
That Is."

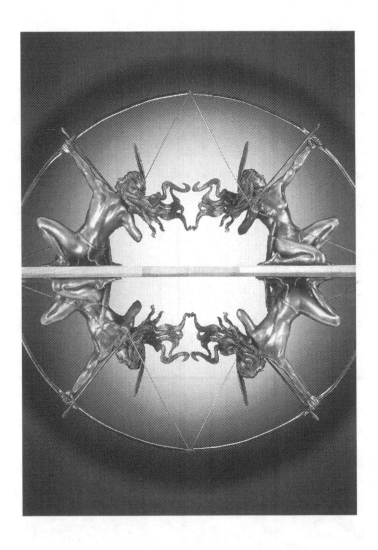

Chapter 5

The Peaceful War

It was still dark in Jaguar's lodge when White Buffalo Woman awoke. Jaguar lay asleep next to her and she curled up close to him, enjoying the warmth of his body. All the challenges of her journey during the past few winters seemed like a faraway memory, and she felt at home in the small lodge.

She got up and lit a tallow oil lamp, then looked around the room. The approach of morning shone dimly through the eastern-facing entrance, and it spilled across the room to illuminate the altar. A beautiful spirit being had been drawn on the wall above the altar, and Buffalo wondered if Jaguar had created this charcoal spirit helper. As she explored the rest of the room, she discovered two skins tied on the northern and southern walls. She lifted one of the skins and found a small opening that looked out toward the horizon where the first glow of twilight showed. She was tying up the skin with the thongs hanging next to the opening when Jaguar sat up, smiling. "I see you have found my little door-looking-outside. I had the idea recently and enjoy gazing out to the sky. But now it is almost time for the sunrise ceremony and we must welcome Father Sun."

As Jaguar stood and began to walk toward the door, Buffalo put her hand on his arm to stop him. "Cat, why it is that you are called Jaguar in your adopted tribe?"

Jaguar smiled and told her how Painted Story had gifted him with a new name of his sacred medicine animal. Although Buffalo could see that this naming was important to him, she could not bring herself to use it. "You will always be Spotted Cat to me, my beloved childhood twin," she told him. Jaguar looked pleased and took her hand as they left their lodge.

While they walked, White Buffalo Woman noticed that the whole village was also gathering at the eastern rim of the Lying Down Mountain. As the sun neared the horizon, the drumming started, and when it finally peeked over the edge of the

Earth, the People lifted their arms and sang a welcoming song. Many birds joined with the villagers, adding their voices to the song of thankfulness for a new day.

After the ceremony, the villagers turned and walked back toward their lodges, now bathed in bright sunlight. On their way back, Buffalo and Jaguar met Hummingbird, who gave them a friendly good-morning hug. White Buffalo's stomach suddenly spun with emotions and she could feel Jaguar's hand tighten on hers. But Hummingbird smiled and spoke in a warm tone. "Come, Buffalo, some women are gathering in the kiva to work on preparations for the upcoming Winter Ceremony." Taking Buffalo's hand, Hummingbird led her to the women's kiva.

As the two women walked hand in hand to the kiva, Buffalo started to relax and feel more at ease. She could understand how Jaguar had become close to this friendly woman. As they climbed to the roof of the kiva, she was excited and reminded of the first time she had entered into the Painted Cave in Gaia for her initiation ceremony. As she descended down the ladder into the kiva, she felt the sense of peace that a sacred place creates.

The female kiva was similar to the men's, but shaped in a circle instead of having four walls. This circle wall was painted with animal and spirit beings. On the altar stood a bowl of water, four ears of corn of four different colors, and carved kachina dolls symbolizing mothers and their children. Many prayer feathers were stuck into the ground around the altar. Grandmother Crow and several other women sat in a circle, and as Hummingbird and Buffalo entered they shifted around to make room for two more.

On the ground in the middle of the circle was a many-colored painting of a medicine wheel. Buffalo looked closely and realized that it was formed of different-colored sands. She wondered how the beautiful wheel was made and how long such a fragile thing could possibly last.

The women sat around the wheel in deep meditation while they tied different objects to prayer feathers. As Hummingbird showed White Buffalo how to create the Sacred Union of Man and Woman prayer feather, she described the meaning of each object. "The wild turkey feather signifies the wildness and mystery of Creation. To this feather, we tie two painted sticks that represent the power of man and woman together in sacred union. The small corn husk bundle containing cornmeal, pollen, and honey symbolizes the nourishment of the spiritual body. Cornmeal represents the physical body, pollen stands for fertility, and honey for the sweetness of love. At the bottom we tie a cord that means long life and a downy eagle plume that symbolizes the breath of life."

As White Buffalo Woman made her first prayer feather bundle, she felt the radiant energy in her hands. Watching the other women, she burned sage and purified the bundle with its smoke. She then offered the prayer feather to the Earth upon the sand painting so it would absorb the power that the Medicine Wheel story contained.

When they had finished tying all the bundles and purifying them with smoke, Buffalo asked Grandmother what they would do with them. "The medicine of the prayer feathers will be put on our kiva altars and on the altars in our homes. Others will be taken out to sacred springs to honor the kachinas that live there. Some will be put into trees in all the Sacred Four Directions around the village to help keep the energy pure and to protect the village from any harm."

The women gathered up the feathers as they sang a medicine song, dancing on the medicine wheel painting until its powers became one with the dancers and the earthen floor. The prayer feathers were placed on the altar, waiting for the next ceremony that would bring them to their new homes.

The women's circle reminded Buffalo of helping Grandmother Spider Woman prepare for one of

the People of the Painted Earth Temple's ceremonies. Although different in form, the medicine
they were creating felt similar to what she remembered in Gaia's Land. She sensed how the prayer
bundles would be a gift of appreciation to the Spirits they were honoring. The kiva gathering brought
back memories of the woman's moon lodge in Gaia.
This friendly circle made White Buffalo Woman
feel as if she were in an adoption ceremony to
become part of a family.

While Buffalo spent the morning with the
women, Jaguar hunted. He had traveled to a place
where sagebrush covered the hills and deer were
plentiful, especially in the early morning. It was
a cool, clear day, perfect for finding the game
he sought. Once he entered the Sagebrush Hills, he
noticed many different trails left by the deer and settled on a set of large prints to follow. As he tracked
the animal, he heard a group of magpies and crows
talking. By the tones of their voices, he knew that
they were enjoying a feast. He guessed that another
village hunter had already found a deer and taken
the meat back to the village, leaving the remainder of
the kill for the birds. He went toward the crow and
magpie meeting to see if he could recognize the footprints of the hunter who had arrived before him.

Over the next hill, he found the recent signs of
a large camp. Many deer had been slain and their

remains were strewn about in total disorder. Only
the choicest part of the deer had been taken, leaving heaps of useful meat still on the carcasses.
Jaguar knew at once that this camp was not a
camp of hunters from his village.

Cautiously, he began to follow the trail left by
this large group of people. He followed it until the
sun was high above his head. Suddenly, he
dropped to the ground. On a high hill in the distance stood a man: a lookout. Staying close to the
Earth, Jaguar crawled through the sagebrush to
get a closer look. Peering through the pale green
plants, he recognized the Nomadic Tribe that had
attacked him and White Buffalo Woman. Jaguar
even recognized the leader of the group as the man
that Buffalo had knocked down when she threw a
well-aimed rock at his head. The hunters were talking, gathered together while the women busily cut
up the deer and cooked the meat. He could understand some of their speech because the men
shouted loudly and signed with their hands when
excited. They were making plans to attack his village the next night.

Stiff with horror, Jaguar wormed his way back
through the sagebrush. As soon as he was away
from the eyes of the lookout, he ran all the way
back to the village. Gasping for breath, he called a
meeting of the tribe.

"We must gather piles of rocks, large fist-sized stones and many small finger-sized rocks. We will place them along the edges of the cliff where it is possible to climb up, and we will put the small rocks in baskets so we can quickly move them to the site of an attack."

While the tribe gathered stones, Jaguar held a brief council with the elders and asked them to prepare for a give-away and a huge feast. He next gathered the hunters together and made plans for a counterattack, teaching them drum signals to coordinate different types of movements and strategies of defense. Finally, he sent scouts to spy out the movements of their attackers.

By the time night had fallen, the whole tribe knew their places and what they would do in the battle to come. The scouts had returned and reported the location of the Nomadics as they approached the Lying Down Mountain. They had chosen a hidden trail, steep and difficult and far from the main trail. The Nomadic People were preparing for a surprise attack at the rear of the village.

Baskets of rocks were rushed to the top of the seldom-used trail. While the last of the attackers began to scale the cliff and the leaders hung in mid-climb, a scout whistled a quick birdcall. Hidden behind the rim of the cliff, every child, grand-mother, man, and woman threw a small stone out into the air. As soon as they threw one stone, they would grab another and another. Their supply was almost endless and the falling rocks became like a huge downpour of rain.

Jaguar was about to cast another stone into the night when he saw stars and realized that a rock had struck the back of his head. Filled with panic that a raging Nomadic warrior had silently scaled the cliff and sneaked up behind him, Jaguar spun around, brandishing his flint knife to meet the enemy. But where the six-foot terror should have stood, three feet of panic-stricken little boy instead stared up at him.

Jaguar let out a sigh of relief and tried to manage a smile through the pain in his head. But the poor child had only seen a gigantic warrior leap toward him, limbs and knives flailing, and disappeared instantly from sight. Jaguar sighed and threw another stone.

Running Dog, the leader of the Nomadic Tribe and Buffalo's attacker, had argued long with his warriors about how to best attack the village. Although it was said that the Peaceful People knew very little concerning war, the main trail was easy for the village to defend. Craftily, he decided to sneak in on the small trail at night and avoid an uphill battle on the main trail.

Running Dog had a new name since a woman had overcome him when she threw a rock at his jaw. His new nickname was Spit-tongue, so named when he spit out the tip of his own tongue and several teeth as well. He had been losing power over his tribe ever since, and to keep control he had told his warriors he would kill anyone who made a sound as they sneaked in. He also mentioned that death would be swift if he ever heard them using his new nickname.

Running Dog felt good as he reached the halfway point up the cliff without hearing a sound. If he could only storm the village by surprise, he might regain some of his lost status with his tribe. But suddenly, a strange hissing sound filled the air and pain shot through Spit-tongue's shoulder where a flying rock had connected. He yelped as numbness shot down his arm.

A roar like thunder came from the ground as a hailstorm of small stones pelted the attackers. The stones were not large enough to cause death or permanent injury, but the warriors felt themselves being bruised and cut. There was no way to escape the pain except a quick retreat down the steep trail.

As a child, Running Dog had earned his name in an incident of which he was rather ashamed: running from a particularly vicious camp dog that had just savagely bitten his behind. He had since earned his fame in the tribe by outstripping everyone in all running events. Now, true to his name and beating all previous records, the leader outfled the entire tribe, including warriors some twenty years his junior.

Once they were winded, the tribe stopped and realized that no one was seriously injured. They could not understand why the village had not used larger rocks in their defense, and as they talked an argument broke out between Running Dog and Summer Deer. Summer Deer favored leading the attack up the main trail, since they were experienced warriors and would eventually win. He again argued his point with Running Dog, who remained obstinately set on his plan.

Suddenly, the tribe was bathed in firelight. Two huge bonfires had flared up nearby, and Spit-tongue yelled his rage that the enemy was attacking. His tribe ran toward the flames, bows out and drawn. But when they reached the fires, they lowered their weapons and stared in disbelief. Between the bonfires was the largest feast any of them had ever seen. Four huge baskets of dried corn were surrounded by big bowls of stewed buffalo, beans, and squash. There were many foods they had never even seen before, like cornbread. Behind the baskets, a spear was planted into the ground and many white eagle feathers fluttered in the wind from its shaft: the sign of peace known throughout the land.

One of the Nomadic men bent down and grabbed a piece of buffalo meat. He took a big bite, and smiled from ear to ear until Spit-tongue hit him over the back with his bow and yelled at him to attack. The feasting warrior shot back, "The white-feathered spear means the village wants to talk of peace. Why should we not eat this offering of goodwill and talk with them?" The rest of the warriors murmured in agreement, for they were very hungry.

Painted Story appeared in the firelight with Grandmother Crow and White Buffalo Woman at his side. "We are the medicine elders of the Tribe of the Peaceful People. We wish to talk of peace between our peoples and give each warrior as much corn as he can carry home."

Despite these friendly words, Spit-tongue drew his bow and aimed at White Buffalo Woman. But before he could loose the arrow, Summer Deer knocked the bow from his hands and threw him to the ground. Several warriors helped to bind his legs and hands and, as an afterthought, his mouth, so they could enjoy their dinner in quiet. Summer Deer then laid down his weapons and lifted his arms, showing his empty hands as a sign of peace.

On both sides of the Nomadic Tribe, Jaguar and the hunters stepped into the light of the fire and put their weapons down on the ground, also lifting their arms in the sign for peace. At last the two tribes sat down together to enjoy the abundant feast, for after the fear and excitement of battle they were all quite hungry.

Chapter 6

The Feasting Relations

Word of the feasting spread throughout the village and soon everyone was heading to where the bonfires blazed. As the grandparents and children arrived at the feast, they were met by another group of people. The women and children of the Nomadic Tribe had also received news of a feast, and soon the meeting had become a great celebration.

By the end of the meal, both tribes were laughing and joyful and becoming pleasantly full of corn honey cakes. The Nomadic children were delighted with this new food and even more delighted to watch Running Dog eat while forced to feast with his hands still tied together. When everyone could eat no more, Grandfather Painted Story spoke. "This is a time of thankfulness and becoming friends. If our meeting had become a war, we would now be mourning the death of people we love. Many hearts would be full of hate toward those who caused the death of a family member. But because we have turned away from war, all in this circle, from the children to the grandparents, have been blessed in this coming together."

Summer Deer rose up and faced Painted Story. "I will speak for the Wandering People, since we have all agreed that Running Dog is no longer our chief. He has brought much bad counsel to our tribe and almost led many of us to our deaths. He has also wronged your people, so I give his fate to you, Grandfather. What will you have us do with him?"

Painted Story closed his eyes briefly in contemplation. "This man is bad medicine and should never be allowed to harm either of our tribes again. It is good medicine that no one has died this night, and I know that the powers would like this blessing to continue. We will banish him forever from the lands used by both our tribes. Only his family may accompany him if they wish. Warriors from both our tribes will accompany him to the lands of the east, and if he ever returns to our territories he will be slain. Also, I would advise you to keep his hands bound until you release him, for he has proven treacherous."

Three women and a girl of eleven winters came up beside Summer Deer. "We are the wives of Running Dog and we do not want to go with him. He has never shown us any kindness and we would rather stay with our tribe." Spit-tongue scowled at this news and spat out a command, although with the recent loss of his tongue tip, it proved less than effective: "Thittle Twee, come wif me!"

But despite the laughter surrounding her, Little Tree trembled with fear and started moving toward him. Hummingbird stepped between them and looked deeply into Little Tree's eyes. "You do not have to obey Running Dog's orders anymore. All your family surrounds you now and they will support your decision." Little Tree threw her arms around Hummingbird's neck, and between muffled sobs on her shoulder Hummingbird could hear her cry, "I never want to see him again!"

Painted Story chose two hunters from each tribe to lead Running Dog to banishment. Jaguar walked to face him and their eyes locked together. Keeping his gaze fixed on Spit-tongue's face, he wrenched his stolen flint knife from the banished leader's belt. He then stepped aside and let the hunters tie a rope to Running Dog's bound hands to lead him away toward the twilight in the east.

Grandmother Crow moved into the center of the gathering. "The Peaceful People would like to gift you with more than corn for your winter's meals. Corn is good medicine for your bodies, and likewise ceremony is good for your spirit. We will show you how we honor the Sacred Powers of the Earth and Sky with ceremony. First, we start each day with an honoring to Father Sun for all his many blessings."

The Peaceful People turned toward the rising sun as their drumming echoed across the land. They sang the morning song and the Wandering People joined in with them. After the sunrise prayers, White Buffalo took out the sacred pipe and led them in the Making of Relations ceremony, explaining each part of the pipe ceremony to her new relatives.

Several of the Peaceful People climbed back to their village and soon returned with many baskets full of corn. Grandmother Crow raised her hands over the baskets in blessing.

"Children of the Corn Maidens, you have been in our hearts and ceremonies for an entire cycle of seasons. We have shared our songs and enjoyed a close relationship with you. May our blessings let you know that we appreciate your life force that flows into us. Go now and join with the Wandering People, who have this day become our relations.

I ask now that four of your medicine people stay with our tribe as our guests. We will teach them how we maintain a relationship with the kachinas. When they sit with us as we create our winter ceremony, they will learn useful rituals that may be incorporated into your winter ceremonies.

It is possible that parts of our stories can join with your own tribal myths. In this joining, you may make a closer relationship with the kachinas of the Corn, the Earth, the Weather, and the Seasons. When you plant corn seeds next spring, the new ceremonies will help you create an abundant new generation of corn with the kachinas.

You should gather together and agree upon which camping place brought you the most joy. In the lands to the south, you must ask part of your tribe to settle in one place, since in order to grow corn you will need a village where people can nurture your corn plants. My friends, try not to move too far from us. We would like to share with you the corn-growing skills that the Powers have taught to us."

From the Wandering Tribe, four people were chosen to stay: Grandmother Sage, the tribal healer who used plants in her healings, Grandfather Finder of Animals, who could dream a good direction for hunting, Summer Deer, who longed to learn more about ceremony, and Little Tree, who wanted to learn about healing plants. The rest of the Wandering People bid farewell to their new relations and, lifting the heavy baskets of corn onto their backs, started walking toward the south. The four who remained watched their families walk away, then slowly turned back toward the Lying Down Mountain.

White Buffalo Woman began to relax and breathe deeply as she walked hand in hand with Jaguar. The image of the People of the Painted Earth Temple lying dead and wounded had haunted White Buffalo Woman since Cat had brought the news that they would be attacked.

White Buffalo Woman saw how skillfully Cat had planned a peaceful solution to the attack. She was very proud of her mate as a powerful war leader who could also listen to his peace-loving teachers.

White Buffalo had great respect for her new medicine teachers and how they had cooled the heat of war that Spotted Cat had brought to the village with his warning of the attack. They had shown him a possible fork in the trail that was leading the tribe into death, destruction, and war. She saw that two trails are always offered, and it takes as much courage to travel toward peace as to go to war.

White Buffalo Woman put her arms around her beloved Cat in a hug as they walked toward the village. She was joyous that he was becoming a wise and mighty chief.

As they approached the village, Grandmother Crow took them to the woman's kiva, along with Painted Story, Tree, and Hummingbird. Little Tree clung to the arm of Hummingbird, who had already decided that she would adopt the young girl. After they had climbed down the ladder into the kiva, Grandmother Crow instructed them to sit in a circle.

"In our village we have built several of these sacred lodges that we call 'kivas,' or worlds below. Each one is dedicated to a certain Spirit Power, which our tribe calls a kachina. We created this particular kiva lodge to honor the sacred feminine powers of women, but actually, all of our kivas hold the power of the Sacred Womb of the Earth. When we enter a kiva during our underground ceremonies, we are returning into our Mother, and when we crawl up the ladder into the air, we are birthing into the world the medicine we created in the Earth's womb.

Recently, we performed a ceremony by creating prayer feather bundles, which you can see on the altar. Soon they will take their medicine to other places where our Winter Ceremony needs their help. Later, Hummingbird will teach you how to make this type of prayer feather. She will explain why each element is needed and how we must meditate on each power as we add it to the bundle. These little helpers carry the power of 'children to be born.'

When we return to this kiva for our Winter Ceremony, the villagers will bring the kernels of the most productive ears of corn that we produced. A large basket will be set on the altar and all the corn will be placed in it. During the ceremony, a young maiden will sit on the basket to help bring the seeds to life. She is like a bird sitting on her nest to hatch her eggs and hasten their birth. At the close of the Winter Ceremony, the corn will be divided and taken to each lodge in the village. Each handful of blessed corn is added to everyone's seed corn to spread the blessings through our gardens.

Into the Winter kiva will come all the spirit helpers that grow the corn stalks with us. People dressed in the spirits' symbolic powers will honor the kachinas by wearing beautifully crafted painted masks and costumes made by our tribe. The dancers represent the spirit beings and become a radiant channel that the transcendent powers can flow through. When the kachina dancers begin to move in ceremony, they often feel the presence of the spirit power joining with their bodies.

There are many different Kachina powers needed in our gardens, and we try to include them all. The Wind, Rain, Sun, Earth, Cloud, and Lightning Kachinas are some of the powers that we invite. Animal, Bird, and Insect Kachinas are also brought into the kiva. Some insects are helpful in the pollination of our crops, though others are harmful and need to be asked to stay away.

Finally, the Sun Kachina will dance to the Grandparents of the Four Directions, asking them for the blessings of their powers to help the stalks grow. The Sun Kachina will also dance for rebirth, because he has diminished since the Summer Solstice and his death comes in the time of the longest night. Out of the darkness he is reborn to grow and increase until his full power comes during summer.

The corn seeds will also die in the Earth to be reborn into the light of their Father Sun. The spirits that were sleeping within the seeds will be awakened and become green Corn Maidens, reaching toward the Sky and the Sun. The Wind Kachina will touch the Green Maidens' pollen stalks, carrying the germinating force to the budding ears and making them pregnant with new life. The Corn Maidens will then birth their life-giving children. Within the ears of corn rest new seeds, completing the circle of death and new life.

All the kachina powers that help us grow corn need to be honored, encouraged, and appreciated. The Winter Ceremony allows us to show respectful kindness and love to all of our helpers on the Path of Life. As all of us sitting in this circle like to be appreciated for our work and gifts, so too do the kachina powers like to be appreciated for their work and gifts to us. This ceremony gives us the opportunity to have a loving relationship with all the powers of creation."

The medicine teachers from the Peaceful People and the Wandering Tribe sat in silence. Each person in the circle could feel a connection with All of Life, and then knew that the coming Winter Ceremony would celebrate the new life that is forever being born into this world.

Chapter 7

The Dream Catcher

White Buffalo Woman sat holding her baby girl in her arms. She rocked gently back and forth as Spider Girl fell asleep with Buffalo's nipple in her mouth. Out of all the moments of her life's journey, it was in this one that she felt her greatest sense of contentment.

Cradling her sleeping daughter, she let her thoughts drift over her life in the New Lands after she had been reunited with Jaguar. Since she had arrived at her new village, a whole cycle of seasons had passed and last moon another Winter Solstice Ceremony had been completed. Spider Girl had been born in the autumn and was now four moons old.

According to custom, the Peaceful People kept their newborn babies inside the lodge for twenty days after their birth. On the twentieth day, White Buffalo Woman had taken her baby outside to the Morning Ceremony. Grandmother Crow, Story, and Jaguar stood together, facing the soft glow of twilight. As the drumming and singing began, Buffalo held the little baby girl up toward the sun, which was just peeking over the horizon. When the baby saw the light of the sun for the first time, Grandmother gave a blessing. "Father Sun, here is your new daughter. Bless her with your gifts of life, helping her grow in strength and power."

White Buffalo Woman felt very comfortable with the ceremonial life of the Peaceful People. Often, the Sacred Powers were honored in ways similar to those of the tribe of her birth. Grandmother had taken Buffalo as her apprentice, and the stories of Turtle Island were merging with the stories of the People of the Painted Earth Temple. She felt that her teacher in Gaia's Land, Grandmother Spider Woman, had somehow seen into the future and known of this coming together.

Crow often questioned her about the teachings from Gaia's Land. Her new Grandmother held Buffalo in great respect as a priestess, for she had been trained in a tradition dating back to both of their tribes' ancestors. It was Crow who had called together this circle of friends and family to attend her baby's name-giving ceremony. This naming was blessed by a medicine sign that came only a few moons after her birth.

On the day of this blessing, Buffalo was away and Jaguar watched their daughter in their lodge. He was busy straightening his arrows while the baby slept on her furry skins. Jaguar was very intent on his work, holding the arrow close to his eye and gazing down its length. He would slowly spin the shaft to see if there were any bends. If he found any, he dipped the crooked arrow in water and bent it straight by passing it over a series of small grooves carved into a flat, heated rock. The arrow shaft would hiss with steam as it was straightened. But this time over the hiss, he heard the baby start to giggle and looked over at her as she awakened.

Chills ran up his back and he felt frozen to the floor. The baby girl held a brown recluse spider by one leg. She was letting the poisonous spider tickle her nose and eyes with the other seven legs. Laughing joyfully, she touched her mouth and then her ear with the squiggly legs.

Jaguar remembered that one of the tribe's hunters had been terribly scarred when one of these spiders had bitten him on the face. He had rolled over onto the spider while asleep and, feeling the sharp sting of its bite, had jumped from his bed in a sickening agony. He was ill for days and the skin around the bite had entirely died away, leaving a deep scar. After he recovered, the hunter's name had been changed to Marked by Spider.

Jaguar was terrified that the spider's bite would kill such a small baby, but the brown recluse almost appeared to be enjoying the play. Jaguar hesitated to grab the spider; that might cause it to bite her face. He sat trembling while he watched the baby's play. Finally, after moments that seemed like entire seasons, the baby girl dropped the spider onto her belly and it scurried down her little leg onto the ground.

White Buffalo Woman would not allow Jaguar to kill spiders in their lodge because she said it would dishonor their Grandmother. So, as he usually did, he scooped up the spider in a small gourd and ran for the door. But forgetting to duck under the shoulder-high opening, Jaguar bumped his head and dropped the gourd on the floor. The spider was much harder to catch the second time; he pounded the overturned gourd over and over on the floor, trying to trap the fleeing creature and listening with increasing irritation as his daughter giggled gleefully. At last successful and holding the precious gourd tightly to his chest, he walked more carefully to the door this time, moving until he was a safe distance from the lodge and releasing the spider onto the ground.

Jaguar ran back to his home as fast as he could and scooped up his little child in his arms, holding her close to him. His heart pounded as he carried her to Grandmother Crow's lodge. Grandmother was working in front of her house, grinding corn by rubbing a long round rock upon a flat stone. A stack of corn stood in front of her, and she was slowly transforming the pile into cornmeal.

Jaguar excitedly told Crow what had just happened. She smiled and told him, "Big medicine has come into your family today. We have been waiting for a sign from the kachinas that would help us name your new baby, and this is surely the one. She is born with Spider as her medicine helper."

White Buffalo Woman was awakened from her fond memories of this medicine naming when Spider Girl pulled on her hair. Looking into her daughter's eyes, she remembered something that Grandmother Spider Woman had said long ago before her journey to the New Lands. She had told Buffalo that although she would remain in Gaia's Land, she felt they would one day be together again.

In the stories of the People of the Painted Earth Temple, it was said that after death the spirit of a human could return to a tribe when it joined with a newborn baby. White Buffalo Woman gazed deeply into her baby's eyes, searching for a glimpse of her Grandmother.

She thought about her initiation ceremony, held so many years ago in the Cave Temple. In that ceremony, Grandmother Spider Woman had gifted her with an ivory necklace of beads and a carved crescent moon. She still wore the treasured gift around her neck. As Buffalo thought about the necklace, Spider Girl let go of her hair and grabbed the ivory crescent moon. Buffalo's whole body tingled as she snuggled the little baby to her breast. She now understood in her heart that she was also embracing Grandmother Spider Woman.

Her little girl would soon receive her medicine name. Calf thought about how she received her name in the Painted Temple tribe. Her father, Falcon, hunted alone one day and saw the footprints of a bison. Usually, several hunters would work together when hunting these large and dangerous animals. Even though he was alone, Falcon decided to see if he could get a good opportunity to use his bow safely and followed the trail.

When Falcon saw the female bison, she was facing away from him and had afterbirth on her backside. The bison had her head down in the grass licking the newly born calf as he crept around for a side shot. He carefully and quietly climbed a nearby tree to take a shot from the safety of its branches. Finding a good perch, Falcon slowly drew his bow. He aimed two hands' width above the bison's heart so the steep angle of his arrow would travel into the body and penetrate the animals heart. As he started to relax his fingers on the string, the calf stood up. Falcon lowered his bow in amazement—the calf was white.

The baby wobbled to its mother on unsure legs and began to nurse. Falcon realized at once that he had been blessed with a medicine sign. He climbed down from the tree and walked toward the village. As Falcon approached his lodge, Grandmother Spider Woman was just leaving. He excitedly told her about his encounter. Grandmother beamed a smile, "You have just become the father of a baby girl and the spirits have given you her name: White Bison Calf."

That night, Grandmother Crow, Painted Story, Hummingbird, Little Tree, Jaguar, White Buffalo Woman, and her baby gathered in the women's kiva. Joining them from the north were Morning Star and three other hunters from her village, while from the southern tribe came Summer Deer and Grandmother Sage.

A feast was brought into the kiva and the delicious fragrance of the food filled the small temple. Jaguar's mouth watered as the smell of stewed elk and herbs filled the room. Little Tree was excited at seeing the basket of honey corn cakes.

The people sat in a large circle, surrounding the feast and a large collection of objects that represented the many paths a life could take. There were hunting tools for a hunter's path, and weaving tools for those who would love weaving above all else. There was a medicine pipe for the path of the shaman, and many other objects that symbolized the different ways that the villagers could make gifts of their lives to the tribe.

The little baby sat in Grandmother Crow's lap and eyed all of the interesting things in the circle before her. Crow lifted the baby. "Mother Earth, this is your new child. Bestow on her your many blessings. Help her grow like a great tree, with her feet touching the ground and her arms reaching to the sky. Give to her the gift of health and wisdom."

She then carried the baby into the middle of the circle and set her down on the ground. "Little Spider Child, there are many paths to choose from as we walk on Mother Earth. One path will bring you your greatest joy, and you may find the right one only by looking into your heart." Grandmother then returned to her place in the circle.

Everyone in the circle watched the child carefully, wondering what object she would crawl to first and what path her life would take. The baby crawled toward a hunting bow and Jaguar grinned from ear to ear. She then moved toward the basket of healing herbs. Grandmother Sage smiled and nodded her head. But as she reached for the basket, Spider Girl saw something next to the basket and bent down for a closer look. It was a small hoop with woven strings in the pattern of a spider web. From the bottom hung seven swan feathers. She picked up the hoop and turned it over in her little hands, peering at it closely as Grandmother Crow lifted the baby up. "Mother Earth, we sit here in this circle and give-away to all the Powers the name of this new child: Dream Catcher."

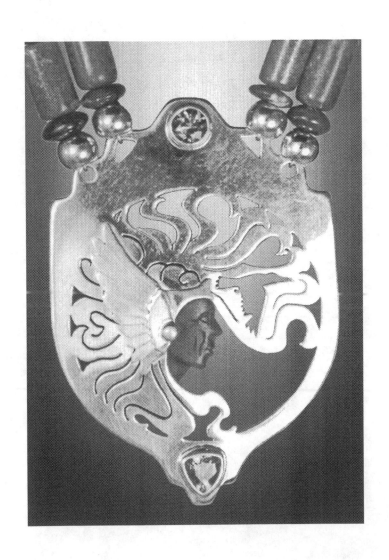

Chapter 8

The Initiation

Spider Girl was very excited. She had just passed through her seventh cycle of seasons and the next ceremony would include her initiation with the other children of her age. For the first time, they would be allowed into the kiva with the kachinas.

Spider had often seen the kachinas during ceremonies in the village. Crow Mother, her favorite, had large crow wings on either side of her head and wrapped herself in a wedding shawl. She sang songs at various shrines throughout the village and then disappeared into a kiva. Sometimes the Powers from the World of Spirit would also bring the uninitiated children wonderful gifts, giving them bows, food, rattles, and even small carved wooden dolls. Once, Spider had been gifted with a doll of Crow Mother, and she treasured this more than any other plaything.

Not all of the kachinas were beautiful and kind. Some were ugly and frightening and dragged children out of their lodges to whip them. It was said that the kachinas knew which children were disrespectful to their elders and would punish them by flogging them with yucca whips.

The initiation rituals inside the kiva were kept secret, though after the ceremony some of the children emerged with bloody wounds on their legs from the whippings. The thought of these wounds on her own legs terrified Spider, although she had never yet been punished by the Whipping Kachinas.

On the evening of her initiation ceremony, Grandmother Crow arrived at Spider's lodge at the time of the new moon. She helped Spider Girl take off her clothes and wrapped her in a white blanket, tying a white eagle feather to the top of her hair. She spoke softly to the trembling girl.

"Dream Catcher, we put a feather in your hair because in this ceremony you are called a baby hawk. After the ceremony, you will be like a young hawk leaving the nest to fly for the first time. The feather also represents your future path: you have shown in your childhood that you will become one of our tribe's spiritual leaders.

When you enter the kiva, the boys will be sitting and facing the girls on the other side of the kiva. Squat on the Earth with your knees at your sides like a baby hawk in its nest. The ceremony will last all night, and for the next several days I will take you home each morning and return you to the kiva each evening."

When they entered the kiva, Spider noticed a sand painting in front of the altar on the west wall. In it, Crow Mother was portrayed, and her presence comforted the girl. She looked around the kiva and saw that a few of the other children also had feathers tied to the tops of their heads. Among those to become the tribe's medicine helpers, she recognized her closest friends.

In the dim light of the fire, she could see many trays of bean sprouts surrounding the altar. The bright green burst of new growth seemed like a breath of spring come into the cold, drab gray of winter. She could see why the people called this ceremony "plant life on a plaque."

Suddenly, a loud noise boomed down from the top of the kiva, like a storm beating at the door.

Three kachinas ran down the ladder, roaring and cackling in terrifying voices. Two held long whips, and the other bore the face of Crow Mother, who yelled to the others to start beating the children. All the children were screaming and crying as they were grabbed and whipped, one by one. Children who had caused trouble in the village were whipped much worse. Through her terror, Spider realized that the Crow Mother Kachina's face was painted with a different design than usual. The violent Crow Mother kept telling the other two to whip harder.

Grandmother Crow sat close behind the shaking Spider Girl and bent to whisper in her ear. "Do not be afraid, Dream Catcher. The children with feathers in their hair will not be whipped."

Spider Girl let out a sigh of relief when the Whipping Kachinas and the false Crow Mother finally left the kiva. Soon, a beautiful song floated through the door of the kiva, and the real Crow Mother descended the ladder, singing. In her hands, she carried a plaque of beautiful green bean sprouts. She also carried spruce, corn, and yucca whips. As she placed these items on the altar, she continued to sing.

The children left the kiva at daybreak and joined in the sun-welcoming ceremony. Spider already felt different from the child who had entered the kiva. She realized that all of the older people of the tribe had been in this ceremony when they were her age, and after several nights the time in the kiva started to feel like a dream. The comings and goings of the colorful kachinas seemed to be ghostly, unreal images.

On the night of the last kiva ceremony, Grandmother again came to fetch Spider Girl from her lodge. The young girl told her teacher about her dreamlike thoughts. "Spider, ceremony is very much like the dream world. The Spirit of Dreams speaks to us in a symbolic language, and ceremony uses a similar way to speak. Every part of this initiation ceremony that our medicine elders have created for us has a meaning. Even if we do not understand everything that happens underground, the things that we experience there are helping us. Your medicine teachers have given you this ceremony to help you become a young adult after being a child for seven winters."

In the kiva that night, more dancers came and went. At midnight, an enchanting song was heard from the top of the kiva. The song spoke of Join Together Kachina running from one sacred spring to another and finally reaching the kiva. Suddenly, Join Together Kachina came sliding down the ladder so fast that it seemed like he had jumped down from the roof. He wore nothing except a breechcloth, and his face was painted black with white spots. Many polished pebbles were tied to his waist and they tinkled like icicles hitting together.

Join Together Kachina jumped upon the sand painting in front of the altar. Singing, he danced on the painting of Crow Mother while she joined with the Earth. Many more kachinas came down the ladder until the kiva became very crowded.

The Spirit Powers danced for the remainder of the night. They danced to the altar and gave their prayer dances to the trays of bean sprouts. Picking some of the bright green plants, they tied bundles to the hair of the children being initiated.

With the arrival of morning the dancing finally came to an end. The Spirit Powers removed their masks, and the children suddenly understood that the kachina dancers were merely villagers impersonating the Spirit Powers. Spider was delighted to see that White Buffalo Woman was the Crow Mother Kachina. It seemed perfect that her mother was the kachina she had always loved most.

Grandmother Crow left her place behind Spider and stood in the middle of the kiva. "You young hawks are now ready to leave this kiva-nest and fly for the first time. Now, you will have more responsibilities in the life of our village. Your elders will teach you to hunt and to work in the cornfields."

"The small children in the tribe will also become part of your responsibilities. Your first duty to the children is to keep what happened in this kiva secret. In order for them to receive the full blessing of initiation, they must come here with an innocent mind."

Women dressed as Bean Maidens now entered the kiva and lifted up the trays of bean sprouts. The initiated children followed them outside, wrapped in their white robes with the green bean plants flowing over their heads. The kachina dancers masked their faces again and followed behind. As the procession passed by the other kivas, they danced around each temple. Out of each kiva came more kachina dancers, who joined in the procession until all the village kachinas were gathered together in the village center.

All of the dancing Spirit Powers were like a beautiful vision and the dancing continued until twilight. As the sky began to darken, the dancers stood still and the drumming stopped. In the silence the many colorful kachinas looked frozen, the only movement being their many feathers fluttering in a small breeze.

The village mothers covered all of the uninitiated children's eyes with their hands. Then the kachinas unmasked themselves and silently returned to their kivas. When the mothers uncovered their children's eyes, the Spirit Powers appeared to have vanished.

After the many nights spent in the kiva during her initiation, Spider Girl felt very comfortable to be in her lodge, lying again on the familiar furs of her bed. She felt much older now that she understood more about the ceremonial life of the village, both above and underground. She felt blessed that she would follow in the path of her mother and grandmother and become a medicine teacher. With this thought, Spider curled up in her furs and drifted into a peaceful sleep.

In her dreams, she found herself dancing with the kachina dancers. As she danced, a huge cloud billowed above the village. A strong wind began whipping her hair and shawl. The sky turned black and sheets of rain hit the village. The wind was so strong that the rain fell horizontally, and when the raindrops pounded on her back it stung from their impact. Lightning burst out of the dark cloud and struck a sacred tree planted next to one of the village's altars. With a loud crack of thunder, the ground beneath her feet shook violently.

With the crash of thunder, Spider awoke with her heart pounding. It took her a long time to drift back to sleep, but when she awakened to sunlight streaming in her lodge's door the dream was pushed back into the corner of her mind. "Oh no! I missed the sunrise ceremony! Now everyone will laugh and tease me." She dressed quickly and ran outside. It was a bright, sunny day and no one seemed to notice that she had missed the ceremony.

A group of six young Bean Maidens approached and invited her to take some of the bean sprouts to a shrine with them. Although the shrine was a far walk through the Valley of Stories and up a side canyon to a sacred spring, it was a chance to get away from the village for the day and she accepted.

The Valley of Stories, its canyon walls covered in mysterious paintings, was Spider's favorite place to walk. It was a warm day for this season and the plaques of bean sprouts were so heavy that the young women stopped often to rest. When they came to the side canyon, she was amazed that she had never noticed the steep climb before. The canyon was only a few steps wide with sheer vertical walls, impossible to climb. As they walked deep into the canyon, the sky became a small trail of blue above the red rock walls. Eventually, the streak of blue widened a bit and the slope of the walls became less steep. Spider noticed footholds cut into the rock face and asked the others about them. They set down their trays of bean sprouts to rest and to view the notches carved into the canyon wall.

Little Tree explained, "The way to climb out of this canyon was made by the Ancient Ones. They lived here long ago before the Peaceful People settled into this land." A blue bird flew out of a bush, beating its wings to climb out of the canyon into the sky. It reminded Spider of something. Suddenly, a clap of thunder shook the ground, and she remembered her dream from the night before about the huge rainstorm. Then she remembered another dream: being in this canyon, a blue bird flying out, then a wall of water rushing down the canyon.

She yelled to the others, "Climb out of the canyon!" She shoved her foot into the first notch and began to climb. She looked down as she ascended the cliffside to see that no one was following her. The other young women looked confused and one protested, "We must take these bean sprouts to the sacred spring." Spider was frantic now. "The spring will come to us; please climb. Quickly!" Little Tree began to follow her and then the others, hearing the urgency in her voice, also started to climb.

Thunder echoed down the canyon and a distant roar grew louder and louder. As the last maiden reached the top of the tall canyon side, a wall of brown churning water came barreling down the canyon. The seven young women stared down as the water ripped through the valley and tore away the bean sprout offerings. If they had remained on the canyon floor, the flash flood would have taken their lives.

Rumor of how Dream Catcher saved the lives of the Bean Maidens spread rapidly through the village. People stared at her with awe. Some of the smaller children became afraid of her glance and murmured about sorcery.

She went to Grandmother Crow and asked her why she had dreamed of something that became real.

"Dream Catcher, you have been blessed with a wonderful gift from the Sacred Powers. Everyone has dreams, and often they are important in discovering how to walk through life in a beautiful way. Some are very gifted in their dreaming and your dream shows that you are one of them. Your dream saved several lives, and someday you may have dreams that could save our entire tribe.

You have an awesome power and some of the villagers may be frightened of you. They may think that you are causing the disasters you dream about. Do not be afraid of this, for your heart is full of love and compassion. I know that you would never

99

do anything that would cause harm to the people or the life on this Earth.

The villagers fear sorcery because it can cause much harm in a tribe. Thinking bad thoughts about someone can be harmful to that person, and thinking bad thoughts with the intention of causing harm can create horrible disruption within a village. A medicine person combining a bad intention and an evil ceremony can sometimes cause a death.

In our village, we teach children not to think bad thoughts about people and there is rarely a problem with sorcery. But in some tribes, sorcery remains a huge problem and the villagers live in constant fear of being harmed by someone's evil intent.

As medicine people, we have a greater responsibility for our thoughts than other people. We must always remember that we have the power to cause healing or harm, and we take a pledge to use our power only for healing within the Sacred Balance. We must never feel arrogant and think we could harm someone with our power for the good of the tribe or ourselves. Such an act would put us on the path of sorcery and imbalance.

Come to me often with your dreams, Spider Girl, and I will share mine with you. Together we may save the tribe from many problems and disasters. Be your namesake and catch your dreams for the benefit of the whole village and perhaps all of life on Earth."

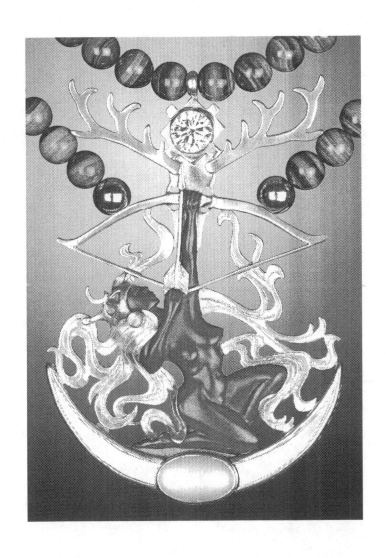

Chapter 9

The Return of Running Dog

Running Dog awoke, staring at the blue sky overhead and watching a few white clouds drift by. Three of his band snored loudly, sounding like wild pigs sniffing out roots. They had feasted last night on a young buffalo they had killed. Hunting had been poor for some time, and they had stuffed themselves until they all collapsed where they sat around the fire. Flies also enjoyed the feast, swarming over the carcass and scraps of the animal nearby.

Dog rolled over and saw that Flicker was also awake. Happy with this discovery, he shouted, "Flicker, bring water to the camp. I am thirsty." The other man grumbled back, "Get it yourself;

you're not crippled." Dog jumped to his feet and grabbed a huge stick, glaring cruelly at Flicker. "I'll beat your skin off if you don't obey the orders of your chief. And after I'm done beating you, I'll kick you out of our band to wander alone until a mountain lion eats you. You'll die out there without your band to support and protect you."

With bent shoulders, Flicker picked up a buffalo bladder and sulked down to the pond. Returning with the water, he handed the bladder to Dog and blurted out, "We need to capture some more women for our band. It has been two moons since the squaw we captured ran off. She probably sneaked away because you beat her so often, Spit-tongue."

Dog snarled back, "I never noticed you treating the squaw with kindness when you had your way with her. In any case, we should not have camped so close to that village. Next time we capture squaws, I will keep them far away from any tribes. It will be easier to control them when there is no village to escape to. And stop calling me Spit-tongue!"

Flicker sat down next to Running Dog. "We should also capture children, for I enjoy having them more than women." Dog grinned back and replied, "So much so that our old tribe banished you into the wilderness. But I agree with you. One of the wives I traded for was only a child when I got her, and it was very energizing to be with her. We should make a plan to capture both women and children."

Spit-tongue thought about Little Tree and his body turned red with rage. His heart pounded, he broke into a sweat, and his entire body burned as his awakened hate surfaced. White Buffalo Woman! All his troubles started when she came into his life. He had lost everything, control of his tribe and his wives, and she was to blame. Flicker was right. If they were to raid a tribe for women and children, it would be the Peaceful People.

"Flicker, we will capture women and children from the Peaceful People. Since they taught you their ceremonies and ways of life, you know all their habits and trails. Think of a time when it would be easy to sneak in and steal Little Tree, White Buffalo Woman, and her child."

Flicker's eyes filled with fear as his body shivered "If we were caught, it would mean our deaths. We must do everything carefully. For an entire moon we should move only at night, without a fire. When we are in sight of the Lying Down Mountain, we will walk only in the creeks or on bare rock to leave no trace of our passage.

"The best time would be harvest time. Everyone picks corn outside the village, and there are many

105

ceremonies that take people into the canyons. The first ear of corn is picked by the grandmother of the tribe and is taken to a shrine far up a canyon. It is given to the spring where water is honored, thanking it for the rain that blessed the harvest."

"Last year, when Grandmother Crow carried the first ear of corn, she was accompanied by Little Tree, White Buffalo Woman, and her daughter Dream Catcher. The three often do ceremony together and they will be carrying large bundles of cornstalks. No men are allowed near this ceremony of the Giver of Rain Spring, so no warriors will be with them. The shrine is a good place for an ambush. I followed their trail last year and sneaked in to look at the shrine: a little pool of water surrounded by cornstalks. They place the first ear of corn in a basket out front."

While he talked, Flicker's eyes widened as he looked at Dog. His hair prickled all over his body as Dog seemed to blur in front of his eyes.

"Don't be afraid, Flick. We will capture them and escape. I am your leader and I will not fail!" With these words he pounded his chest hard with a fist, but a pain shot through his breasts that stunned him. Wait, I have no breasts! Dog stared down at his body, realizing with horror that it had turned into a young girl's body. Then he fainted.

Spider Girl awoke with a start, her small breasts throbbing with pain. The dream was still vivid in her mind and she burst into tears. She hastily dressed and ran to Grandmother Crow. There, she found both her mother and Little Tree already present; between sobs, she described the dream to them in detail. "The feeling of hate in Spit-tongue was overwhelming. I do not understand how anyone could live with such an emotion inside his body. What does it mean, Grandmother? How can a person live with such hate inside himself?"

Grandmother put her arms around Dream Catcher and stroked her hair. "Dear one, I am so sorry you had to experience something so horrid. In my dreaming, I also can enter into another person and experience life from their perspective. It can be very disturbing and strange, since I can dream far into the future or far into the past.

"Your dream is very important and we must be prepared in case it is a true event. Do not fear your dreaming power, for you may again save lives with your gift. Before we talk further, Buffalo, go and bring Jaguar to this council."

Little Tree was trembling with fear. "Grandmother, why would anyone abuse a child? They are so sweet and innocent. How can anyone be so cruel and thoughtless?"

Grandmother put her hand on Little Tree's shoulder to calm her.

"Many people who are very cruel were treated badly as children themselves. This makes their behavior seem natural in their minds. They lie to themselves and ignore the obvious truth of the pain their actions cause. Although they often lie to others, they never stop to realize that it is possible to lie to one's own self too.

Also, it is the very innocence of a child that attracts them. Although it is impossible to describe our existence in the World of Spirit, we could think of ourselves as beings of light. Babies come into the world full of the energy from the other side. We all enjoy holding babies because they are so full of light, and so close to the World of Spirit from where we all come and to where we will all return.

Sorcerers understand this source of great energy and will use the abuse of a child to gather more power into themselves. When they steal a child's fire, they perform the most unbalanced act a human can. It is the most greedy, selfish, arrogant, mean act that one human can inflict upon another.

108

I believe that Spit-tongue is such a person. Although I always try to take the peaceful path, if your dream is true I believe it would be correct to take Spit-tongue's life away from him. He chooses his own end if he returns after being banished. We would also save future children from his abuse. When a dog is injured, we try in every way to heal it, but when a dog has been bitten by a rabid animal and goes mad in its head, we must kill it, for it would injure other animals and people."

At that moment, White Buffalo Woman returned with Jaguar. The parents had discussed their daughter's dream as they walked back to the circle, and now Grandmother Crow spoke to Jaguar. "You have been chosen as our tribe's war chief. You have learned well how to walk the peaceful path of our tribe and yet you understand the ways of war when they are forced upon us. You must form a plan in case the people you love are attacked."

Preparation for the Harvest Ceremony continued as usual. Jaguar thought long about how to both protect the women and children and still create a beautiful and complete ceremony.

Jaguar sat with Grandmother Crow, White Buffalo Woman, and Painted Story in the kiva for four days making prayer feather bundles. People brought in sand from the cornfields and sprinkled it on the floor as part of the altar, and placed painted wooden figures behind the altar, symbolizing the love and reproductive qualities of women. Between them were sticks painted like clouds and raindrops, which represented the Rain Powers of the Four Directions. On the blessed sand sat a bowl of holy water surrounded by four ears of corn: yellow corn to the west, blue corn to the south, red corn to the east, and white corn to the north. Eagle feathers standing upright in the ground completed the medicine helpers.

On the fifth night of the Harvest Kiva Ceremony, Dream Catcher, Morning Star, Little Tree, and Hummingbird joined them, and on the seventh night, Grandmother Crow began to sing the story of creation. Painted Story joined his voice with hers.

"In the beginning, there was only the heavenly Goddess, who was formed out of the endless empty space in which the Creator lived. The Creator wanted to create life and so he made a nephew to help him in Creation. Nephew gathered together and manifested the waters, which he divided into solids and waters. Nephew then formed air

110

that became the winds and breath of life. He did this nine times to create nine Universes.

On the First World, he created a helper to remain on the world and create life. Her name was Spider Woman and she created all the plants and animals. She gathered four types of Earth to use in creating people: yellow soil, red soil, white soil, and black soil. Mixing them with her saliva, she created the humans. She told them to face toward the east as the first sunrise came over the horizon, and said, 'You are meeting your father, the Creator.' The people of the First World were wise and could talk with the animals. They also understood that because they were made from the Earth, she was their mother.

Nephew's helper then created corn to be the food for the humans. The wise humans understood that the Corn Maiden's flesh also became their bodies, meaning that the corn was also their mother like Mother Earth.

Nephew told the people to always walk the world in a balanced way and sing praises to their father, the Creator. The people multiplied but many became very self-absorbed and forgot to sing praises to their father.

reeds and, after putting in a little water and cornmeal for food, sealed the ends. She then got into the last reed with the People and sealed it tight.

Nephew loosed all the waters. Waves higher than mountains rolled over the land. Islands broke and fell under the sea. The People inside the reeds could hear the rushing water and the pounding rain, although they were safe floating on top of the water.

After the Fourth World was created, Spider Woman unsealed the reeds and let the people out on a small island. She taught them to tie many layers of reeds together to make rafts. In small groups, they paddled from island to island until they came to the huge Turtle Island.

When they arrived on Turtle Island, they heard a great noise and saw a man created by Nephew to be the caretaker, guardian, and protector of the land. He said, 'In the Fourth World, your life will be difficult and you will have to labor hard to grow corn and hunt. First, you must separate into your different clans and travel to all the corners of this land. After you have visited and claimed all of Turtle Island, you will return to the heart center of the Turtle and form one tribe again. This time, you must keep your covenant with the Creator and walk in balance with all Creation. Praise your Father and honor your Mother with songs and ceremonies. Remember to appreciate all of life with open hearts while always walking the path of peace. If you forget this covenant, I will again take the Earth from you with a purification that will end all life in the Fourth World. As long as there are some who keep the covenant, a few will survive, even if the world must be purified again."

The eight medicine people sat in silence when the Creation song ended. They all felt the importance of these teachings and all the other parts of the covenant that the Peaceful People still upheld.

They left the kiva while it was still dark and walked to the cornfields. With great ceremony, Grandmother Crow picked the first ear of the new corn. The others then cut large bundles of Corn Maidens to be used in the kachina dances over the following days; but first, some would be left at the Giver of Water spring shrine. Grandmother led the procession into the Valley of Painted Stories, and they walked together in silence as they turned up a side canyon.

Little Tree hoped no one would notice her hands were trembling. Her mouth was dry and her heart was pounding at the thought of meeting Spit-tongue.

Dream Catcher hoped that her dream was not prophetic. Looking around, she remembered another dream. In it, she and the Bean Maidens had almost died in this part of the canyon.

White Buffalo Woman believed that Spotted Cat had thought of all the possible problems with the counterattack. She wished the young girls were not included in his plans even though they would ensure that Running Dog did not suspect trickery.

Grandmother silently prayed to Mother Earth and Father Sky to protect all her children. She felt strange to be leading them into battle and was glad she did not have to carry a weapon.

Running Dog and his band of six followers felt confident. They were certain that no one had detected their entry into the land of the Peaceful People. Flicker had led them into the top of the canyon that held the shrine with its small pool of water, and the band continued down until they came to a place with several large boulders. Here, they set up an ambush.

Seething with hate and feeling the pit of his stomach churn with fear, Running Dog crouched behind a rock. Revenge would soon be his for all the disgrace he had suffered.

They saw Grandmother Crow approach with a basket in her hands, followed by seven women holding bundles of cornstalks. When the group of women had reached the boulders where they hid, Flicker and Spit-tongue jumped out in front of them. The other men slunk out of the shadows on either side, leaning menacingly on their bows and fingering the coils of rope to bind their prisoners. Running Dog and Flicker had arrows notched in the strings of their bows.

Dog sneered. "Hello, Old Gray Hair. At our last meeting you did most of the talking, but this time I am in control. I have decided to silence you forever since you are useless to us, but the others will be taken as squaws."

They raised their bows. Quick as a lightning flash, all the women dropped their bundles of Corn Maidens, revealing drawn bows. Two arrows sang through the air and shot through the chests of Spit-tongue and Flicker, killing them before their bodies reached the ground.

Their leader dead, the rest of the diminished band fled in terror before the warrior women and their bows. They scattered in all directions through the canyon, running for their lives. Had they once looked back, they would have seen that two of the "women" were actually Jaguar and Painted Story in women's clothes.

When Story saw the band running in panic, he held up his hand and the women lowered their bows. He realized that without their false leader, the followers were harmless and lost. Perhaps this near-death experience would set them on their true path of peace, prosperity, and compassion. Also, after the band told stories about the courageous warrioress women, the Peaceful People would be safe from attacks.

Grandmother Crow, though shaken, set down the sacred offering.

"Although we have been forced to make war during the Harvest Ceremony, we must continue. The women and I will walk to the shrine and complete this part of our ritual. The warriors close behind us will soon arrive and take these two men to their final resting place.

Painted Story and Jaguar, see that they are buried in a medicine wheel circle of stones. Plant a peach tree over each man with ceremony. They no longer need these bodies, so let them now nourish new life in the valley below.

Mother Earth, Creator, and helpers in the Spirit World, take these spirits into your

world and help them as they experience all
the pain they have created for other people
during this lifetime. Help them to learn
from the suffering they have caused. In a
future time, let them be healed and learn to
walk in balance on our Mother Earth."

Chapter 10

The Dream Circle

Grandmother Crow and the Corn Maiden Priestesses carried the Corn Maidens as they continued their walk to the spring that fed the small creek that flowed down the canyon. As she knelt on the ground, Grandmother placed the basket with the year's first corn next to the small pool. The stream emerged from a crack in a rock and splashed with the sounds of delicate water music. The Corn Maiden Priestesses formed a circle and placed the cornstalks in a sunburst pattern around the little pond.

Putting a flame to a braid of sweetgrass and cleansing the circle with the smoke spread by her crow-wing fan, Grandmother spoke:

"Sacred Water Spirit, we bring you the first corn in appreciation for your gift of life that has helped her to awaken. You have blessed the seeds we planted in the Spring Ceremony and brought the rains so the Corn Maidens would have nourishment. You have come to our kachina dances when we invited you and our corn has prospered and grown. We thank all the Water Spirits for the abundance they have brought to us."

The priestesses and Grandmother returned to the village later in the day. As they approached, they saw the Peaceful People gathering corn in the fields for the final ceremonial offering. Grandmother's circle had missed this day's important sunrise ceremony. Not wishing Little Tree or Spider Girl to feel left out, she explained the ritual to the two girls.

"The village chief enters the kiva to lead the dancers out for the morning ceremony. He takes one of the women's hands and she, in turn, takes the hand of another woman until all inside hold hands. Although climbing the ladder while holding hands is slow and tedious, it takes mutual cooperation that honors the Emergence of the Peaceful People's ancestors into the Fourth World.

To complete the Harvest Ceremony, the women dancers gather Corn Maidens from the stalks before sunrise and hold them as they dance in the center of the village. There, the other women throw food and gifts to the villagers. The children squeal and laugh as they try to catch peaches, honey cakes, and toys. After the dance, the cornstalks are placed on the ground where the women have given prayers to Mother Earth with their dancing. As the people leave the village center, a member from each household picks up one Corn Maiden and returns home with her. Once placed on the stack of harvested corn inside the house, the Maiden brings a blessing to each household."

As the harvesting corn ceremony ended, Grandmother Crow gathered the seven who had been attacked, and together they entered the Women's Kiva.

"I am sorry you experienced the making of war today, especially Dream Catcher and Little Tree, for you are too young to be a part of such violence. Thankfully, this type of unbalanced behavior is rare on Turtle

Island, and I hope that none of you will again be forced to take a life in the defense of our village.

From the stories White Buffalo Woman has told us, there is much war in Gaia's Land. The Slave Tribes that follow the Thunder God have lost the Sacred Balance and have begun to dominate other tribes. The Earth Goddess is no longer seen to be in equal harmony with the God. These unbalanced people no longer consider how their actions affect Mother Earth and all her Creation.

I would like this council to meet every new moon and discuss the dreams we have had. All who are gathered in this circle have been shown to have powerful dreams, and Dream Catcher has just demonstrated again how important it is to share our dreams with other medicine people. I will begin now with dreams that have recently come to me.

At times, I am able to dream far into the future and observe life near the end of the Fourth World. I believe these dream visions come to me from the Caretaker who was left on Turtle Island to remind us to keep our covenant with the Creator. By seeing what will happen to our future, we can prepare for the drastic changes to come. As the Caretaker said, if we and others like us do not keep the covenant, we and the Fourth World will end.

Yet all the destructive dream visions I have been shown do not have to come to pass. The Fourth World was given to humans so we would be partners with Creation in the unfolding of life on Mother Earth."

Grandmother was silent for a moment while the dreamers in the circle pondered the importance of this newly formed circle. They thought back to their past dreams, wondering if some of them were visions from Caretaker or Spider Woman. They silently resolved to be attentive to all of their dreams from now on.

Hummingbird suddenly remembered a dream.

"Grandmother, several nights ago I had a dream in which I was flying. Flying dreams are my favorite type and when one comes to me, I usually awake relaxed and refreshed. But this dream was very strange.

I was lying on the ground looking at the sky, which was very clear. I heard a distant roar and saw a small, shiny object start to move across the sky. It left a white trail that slowly drifted into a long, white cloud. I wondered what object could be so high in the sky. With this thought, I was suddenly in the sky itself! Looking down, I could see the entire Lying Down Mountain and all the land around for a long distance.

But just as suddenly as I had found myself in the sky, I was in a large room, looking out of a hole in the wall. The hole was covered with mica and I tried to find the Painted Valley outside. Turning to look around the room, I became frightened, for it was filled with many strange people. They were different colors; some were black, yellow, and white, although some were red like our tribe. Their clothes were different from any tribe I have ever seen."

Grandmother smiled.

"I too have seen the trails in the sky. In the future, people will be able to fly in lodges like the one you saw and travel quickly through the sky.

The people you saw came from different lands on the other side of Mother Earth.

When Spider Woman made the people from different colors of Earth, they became the way you saw them in your dream.

You may remember that the people of Aztlán also had flying lodges. As the end of the Third World approached, they became conceited about these creations and lost sight of the fact that they were only a small part of a larger, interdependent world.

I have dreamed that people who emerge dominant from the wars in Gaia's Land will overwhelm Turtle Island. They will be like the People of Aztlán and will try to force their way of life on the Peaceful People. If we wholly give up our way of life and become dazzled by all the exotic creations of these people, then the Fourth World will end in destruction.

But if we can keep our covenant with the Creator, the changes will not be so horrible. It is possible that the passage into the Fifth World could be a time of peace, beauty, and walking in balance. We must teach our children how important it is to have relationships with the kachinas. The ability to call rain to our cornfields is much more powerful than flying though the air in a lodge.

The dominant people from Gaia's land will believe that their race is superior, and they will try to conquer and convert all other races. After they conquer our village with war, they will also want to control our minds. They will try to take away our language, our ceremonies, the way we dress, and what we eat. Even our children will be taken away from us and schooled to think like the dominant people."

White Buffalo Woman spoke next.

"I can now see why you called this Dream Circle together, as I also need to speak of a dream that I have had. I dreamed that spider webs stretched from lodge to lodge and continued to stretch out to trees without limbs. I could see these trees with cobwebs following down large trails until they disappeared from sight.

In my dream, the village looked very different. The lodges were pushed together and even stacked on top of one another. Inside one of the cramped lodges, a woman dressed in strange clothes with tiny flowers painted on them stood by a bowl. Water poured out of a stick into this bowl. Suddenly, I heard a sound like a high-pitched rattle and the woman picked up an object connected to the web.

She started talking to the object while holding it to her ear. I traveled along the web string and came to another lodge where another woman talked to a similar object. They were having a conversation from one side of the village to the other."

Grandmother seemed to be in deep thought. "We must add this to our story of the future of our village. Our people will speak through cobwebs. Does any more of your dream seem important, Buffalo?"

Buffalo answered:

"Yes, although it is difficult to describe. I followed the web to another lodge and saw a man sitting on a large, colorful, soft bed. There, I began experiencing life though this man's eyes.

He was staring at an object with a small mica-covered hole in it. The hole had an eerie light and, as I looked closer, I saw moving people in it! It reminded me of the pictures we see in our imagination. But inside the object that showed moving pictures, the people spoke in a language from another tribe and treated each other violently. Suddenly, the picture changed and became a forest with animals passing through it.

The man was very round and weighed almost as much as two normal villagers. His mind was nearly asleep while he watched the moving pictures. The pictures were portraying a person's life story that was, in his mind, his own experience. He was staring dully and allowing the pictures to live out his life without ever leaving the large bed. He did not feel like interacting with other humans or animals. In fact, his huge size would make hunting or even walking very difficult.

I felt a deep sense of sadness in the man of the future. He had lost contact with the Earth and the growing of corn. He had no relationship to or appreciation for the food he was eating, and the grains and meat he consumed held almost no life force in them. He had no experience of the joy of hunting and the relationship of the give-away.

I awoke from this dream crying from hopelessness. The future man from our tribe had allowed himself to be cut off from the wisdom of his mind and the wisdom of his body. His life held neither purpose nor joy."

White Buffalo Woman set down the talking stick in the middle of the circle, and Grandmother Crow picked it up. "We can now see how important it is for this Dream Circle to meet each new moon. Although it will be difficult for us to keep our traditions alive in the future, we are the medicine teachers of the Peaceful People and we must start preparing for the time of great changes. Although they may be more than an entire Age away, we will encourage our people to stay connected to the natural environment and the covenant with the Mother and Father of Creation."

Chapter 11

The Touch of Winter

The touch of winter reached out toward the Lying Down Mountain. The Peaceful People watched the crescent moon become smaller each night, and soon the birth of the new Moon of the Hawk and the first ceremony of the year would be upon them.

"Germination Manifest" would mark the celebration of the Creative Fire with which life begins. Grandmother Crow had postponed the next Dream Circle until after the sixteen-day ceremony. The first eight days were given over to preparing prayer sticks and purifying the participants, who would reenact the intricate story of creation in the second half of the ceremony. The kiva dancers would play many different roles, carefully remembering and honoring the sacred story.

Grandmother invited Dream Catcher to the last ceremonial morning in the kiva. Night was still falling as the two entered the cool darkness of the kiva. Soon, Spider Girl could hear others descending the ladder and gathering in the silence. Grandmother spoke into the black void. "In the dawn of creation, before there was light, the first fire was kindled. It impregnated all forms of life on Earth. The plants, the animals, and the humans became manifest after this germination from the light."

A clashing sound broke the silence and sparks danced out of the darkness. In the quick flashes of light, Dream Catcher saw a kachina with two long horns striking flint stones together. The kachina sat in front of the fire pit, which held cotton fibers onto which the sparks fell. She also noticed that the altar now held a huge set of elk antlers. In front of the antlers sat a small carved man, surrounded by many beautiful and intricate prayer sticks.

As a small flame appeared in the cotton fibers, she realized that there were many kachina dancers in the dim light. Grandmother's voice again broke the silence.

"As the Upper World becomes bathed in twilight, we honor the first fire in the Under

World. Let it now awaken these prayer sticks on our altar, each of which celebrates a different aspect of life. The first prayer stick celebrates Father Sun and calls him into our ceremony. The second offers thanksgiving to the vegetation, especially the primary corn, squash, beans, and tobacco plants. The third represents the many blessings of the animals and humans, and the fourth prayer stick symbolizes the Earth as she expands under the warmth of the sun.

The Creative Fire with which all life begins has now been honored. As we leave this kiva, let us remember the Emergence from the Under World of our ancestors. This first ceremony of the new cycle of seasons we give to the germination of all forms of life on Earth. The course of her development has been laid out."

Three kachinas placed embers from the now-blazing fire into small bowls. They climbed up the ladder to take these children of the First Fire to the other three kivas that were helping in the ceremony. Later, after the public kachina dance, the kachinas would bring brands of the First Fire to relight the hearth fires of all the village's lodges.

Once everyone had left the kiva, two kachina dancers closed the paths that led into the village with two lines of cornmeal. There, they stood guard to ensure that no one would enter the village this day and night. Only one path was left open for the spirits to enter the village, and a feast had been prepared for them in all of the eastern lodges. The villagers left these lodges empty and went to lodges on the western side of the village.

All villagers stayed indoors that night, gathered in the western lodges with the doors tightly shut as the spirits entered the village and enjoyed the feast. Inside, the people performed purifying ceremonies by washing each other's hair with yucca suds while the kachina dancers walked the outside paths to ensure that no one would disturb the spirits.

In the morning, the villagers were permitted to watch the kachina dancers from the open doors of the west lodges. Once the dancers had finished they stood still in front of the lodges, where everyone was now very tired of being cooped up in the crowded rooms. With a burst of coyote yells and laughing, the last part of the ceremony began in a climactic burst. The village women ran out of the lodges into the winter morning with bowls of water and drenched the dancers to purify them. Then the cold, wet, dripping dancers turned and walked back to their kivas.

That afternoon, Grandmother Crow gathered the Dream Circle together and they entered into the Women's Mysteries Kiva.

"I believe that our circle may be the most important give-away we will perform in our lifetimes. Now, we must do more than discuss our dreams of the time of great changes: we must also warn the future generations of the Fourth World.

We must leave instructions for a balanced pattern of life for the people, since most of them will lose all touch with the natural Balance of Life during the end of this age. Within this Dream Circle, we know the joy and experience of being part of all life on Earth. We need to share this wisdom in stories that can be passed down through the cycles of seasons to help guide our children's children to the end of this age."

Little Tree picked up the talking stick.

"In my dreams of future time, I woke up experiencing life through a young woman's eyes. She lived in a lodge made of iron and mica, and many lodges were stacked on top of hers in a pile as high as a mountain.

When I looked outside, I could not see the end of the lodges as they stretched out in all directions.

Many objects ran over the large trails below me, and I was so high in the sky that the people below looked like swarms of ants. A horrible noise roared everywhere and hurt my ears. When I opened the mica covering the hole and took a deep breath, the air burned my lungs.

The woman looking out into her great village was troubled. She worried about something called 'money,' which the people in her village traded for food. She hated an activity called 'work' she had to do to trade for this 'money.' She had to do meaningless things all day in a small room without seeing the sky, but she was in much fear of not doing the 'work' and having to live outside with no food.

In this one great village lived more people than there are in the entire world at this time. They grew no food in the village, for they had covered all the land with sheets of stone. There were no animals to hunt and the water in the river was unhealthy to drink. She felt like she was not living, only existing."

Morning Star was next to speak.

"The objects that Little Tree saw moving along the trails have also been in my dreams. The future people form small lodges out of metal. Underneath, medicine hoops turn between the lodge and the ground, and these sacred circle symbols move the metal lodges along the ground.

   The people sit in these lodges so they do not have to walk from one place to another. I watched as some of them left through a small door in the moving lodges. They were weak and frail because they so seldom used their muscles. Grandmother, how can these people understand stories that we pass down from our lives? Their view of us will be as confusing and difficult to understand as their life is to us."

Grandmother paused for a moment, then replied:

"The Peaceful People seem capable of keeping the covenant with the Creator better than any other tribe I have ever experienced. If we can help our tribe stay on this path, they may become the ones who can teach the future People.

We see in our dreams how miserable people will become, and certain ones may look to the Peaceful People for answers to why their lives seem so sad. With our help, our tribe's prophecies will carry stories of future events and when our children's children watch them coming true, they will honor the stories of their ancient ancestors. They may see our stories as a way to live a good life through the difficult times. When people become more highly removed from life and careless, there will always be some who recognize the destruction around them. They may seek a good path to follow and, in doing so, discover the Way of the Peaceful People."

Grandmother laid down the talking stick in the middle of the circle of medicine people, where Dream Catcher reached out for it.

"This Dream Circle has stimulated me to dream more and more about the future of our tribe. From my visions, I worry that our children will abandon the covenant with Creation.

In my dreams, I see the children near the end of the Fourth World turning away from the Sacred Balance of the Peaceful People's life. Boys and girls are wearing clothes that offend their parents. They are not helping in the cornfields or learning the ceremonies, and some of them have no respect for the tribal elders. Many do not even bother to learn the tribal language and have been totally absorbed by the dominant culture.

These children are so distracted by new inventions and food that they laugh at their elders. They feel like their own parents are their enemies. Strangely, though, I also see young people from the dominant culture who do have respect for the elders. They come to learn from our future medicine teachers and, in time, know more about our ceremonies and way of life than some of our own children's children. They are eager to help the Peaceful People and learn all they can about ancient prophecies and ceremonies."

Grandmother smiled and replied,

"Dream Catcher, I am happy to hear your dream, for it confirms the visions within my own dreams. Not all of the people who come from across the Great Water will be unbalanced. White Buffalo Woman and Jaguar both came from Gaia's Land but have still contributed so much to our community. As your Grandmother, I say that our wisdom and teachings will be open to all people who wish to walk the path of the Sacred Balance and the Way of Peace.

Soon, we will come into the time of our Winter Solstice Ceremony and embrace the spirit of this introspective season. In the teachings that we will pass on to our future family, let us stress the attitude that we hold during this season within our ceremony.

This is a time when we pray for the entire world and prepare the atmosphere for the whole year. We try to use only wholesome words, which uplift and cause no harm. It is a time of teaching children to respect others, guarding against disturbing behavior. We talk to loved ones about the past, present, and future while reviewing the divine laws. We contemplate how our Mother Earth is a living being who feels and responds, and we examine our conduct during the past year in order to make improvements. We remember the Sacred Powers and ask them for their loving care and rain.

We must be clear and disciplined about the attitudes and intentions that we bring to our ceremonies. If we only pass the rituals and forms of our ceremonies on to the future, they will not be whole. We must also convey that in ceremony, attitude is always an equal partner with application."

Chapter 12

The First Robin

hite Buffalo Woman awoke before twilight. She lay staring into the blackness, wondering why she had arisen so early. A bird sang in the distance, anticipating the soon-to-come sunrise: a lone robin greeting the day. *A robin!* Buffalo suddenly realized. *The first robin!* The southwest winds had brought unusually warm days with springlike weather. Buffalo's heart filled with joy, and she decided that today the family would walk to Waterfall Meadow.

When dawn appeared, she looked outside and saw two robins nearby, playing excitedly at mating. Something woke up in Buffalo's body, and soon she was daydreaming about the meadow and expanding her plans for the day.

By the time Spider Girl and Jaguar awoke, she already had a basket of food packed for a day outside and away from the village. Jaguar realized at once that his plans to go hunting would have to change, and Spider became bouncy at the thought of spending an entire day in the beautiful meadow.

When they reached the meadow, the field glowed as though it radiated its own light. Buffalo and Jaguar lay in the new grass, surrounded by the first small yellow flowers of spring. Spider ran after a butterfly toward the waterfall and Buffalo knew she would be gone a while, watching baby frogs in the water.

When the sun was close to setting, it was difficult for them to tear themselves away from the peaceful beauty of the place. "Cat, it is hard to imagine all the horrible events we discuss in our Dream Circle. Why can't people see how beautiful life is?"

Jaguar lay on his back with a smile on his face and a warm glow in his body, wishing they could spend the night in the meadow.

"I know how you feel. The stories of our medicine teachers and our own experiences tell us that unbalance is part of our passage on Mother Earth. The first three worlds have set a pattern that the Fourth World already seems to follow.

146

Our teachers also say that humans were given the power to co-create the future of life on Mother Earth. I am sure the people in our dream circle have the power to change that future. I believe that if enough people try to create peace and harmony, the Web of Life will shift and war and discord will fade away."

That night at the Dream Circle, Jaguar was first to speak.

"In my dream, the leaders and traders of the world became more and more greedy. They caused conflicts between different peoples for their own profit and power. The rich people never had enough and kept acquiring more, while the poor always had less and less. Whole tribes were starving, even though the accumulated food was enough to feed all humans.

Eventually, the gap between people became too wide, and all around the world the people in poverty banded together to fight for equality. The war was horrible. They used sticks that made a sound like thunder and threw a small arrow a great distance, but the other side dug pits in the ground to escape the little arrows. Another weapon poisoned the air around the pits, and many warriors who thought they had found safety died, choking from its poison.

Despite the poor people's uprising, the same powerful leaders and traders still controlled this war to end all wars. Nothing changed, and there soon came a second war, again involving most of the people in the world.

The second war began involving two nations of people who used sacred symbols to lead their warriors: the symbol of the sun and a cross of four sacred powers turning in a circle. Flying lodges were used to drop thunderbolts of fire onto people below. Warriors also dropped from the sky like rain.

This war finally came to an end when a flying lodge dropped the largest thunderbolt of fire ever created. A huge gourd-shaped cloud formed beneath it, filled with hot ashes that killed everything in an area bigger than Lying Down Mountain. The ashes boiled the land, killing all plants, insects, birds, animals, and humans. Even the soil died, and nothing could grow.

Finally, the leaders and traders, who had become even more rich and powerful by this time, caused a third war. But this time, both sides possessed the gourd-of-ashes weapon and most of the life on Mother Earth was destroyed."

Painted Story sighed as Jaguar passed the talking stick to him.

"I too have seen the three great wars in my dreams, but I saw that two paths existed: one leading ever closer to the Great Purification and one toward peace. If the path of war is always chosen, the third war might become the way that the Fourth World is cleansed, ending most of the life on Mother Earth.

After the first great war, the leader of Turtle Island will try to create a peace council of all nations. He will fail, and only after the second great war will the peace council be formed.

It will be housed in a council lodge built next to the Great Water, facing the rising sun. The lodge will be as tall as a small mountain and built of iron and mica, able to hold many tribes of people at once.

The council will talk about peace and will do much to help the poor and starving tribes of the world. Although the struggle between the rich and poor will continue, it is possible that peace could be chosen at this time."

Dream Catcher picked up the talking stick as Grandfather set it on the ground.

"In my dreams, I am usually with our tribe during the great wars. There is less and less interest in our traditional ceremonies, though they manage to continue.

Eventually, I see the nation of Turtle Island become the most influential power in the world. They try to overwhelm all the tribes of the world with their way of life, and the Peaceful People continue to take refuge at the heart of Turtle Island: the strongest medicine place for helping the world choose the path of peace. Even if all the tribes lose their traditions, the Peaceful People will be the last tribe to do so.

My dream helpers remind me always to remember the children in our attitudes, ceremonies, warnings, and instructions, for the future will always be in their hands. Grandmother Crow, what instruction can possibly help children born into the chaotic times? How can they find balance toward the end of the Fourth World as we have experienced it in our dreams?"

Grandmother took the talking stick.

"Dream Catcher, the wisdom you express is far beyond your eight winters. In my dreams, I see time and space start to vary as the fabric of the world starts to tear. Time will appear to move faster and confuse the people. The leaders and traders will try to destroy the last of the wild natural places, but many people will recognize the need to preserve these places and the plant and animal families that are disappearing. They will sense that every time one species ends, there will be less power to hold the fabric of life on Mother Earth together.

During this time, each person must seek out one of the wild and natural places still spared from destruction. When they spend time alone experiencing the balance of nature, an ancient memory will awaken. Once they return to the artificial human-made world, they will see the imbalance with a whole new vision.

In the wild, they will relearn the interdependence of all life and their relationship with it. Our children's children will relearn that water is alive, and they will learn to honor the life that joins with them when they drink. In the plants and animals that give-away, they will also feel the sharing of life gifted to humans.

When the future people return to their houses of iron and mica, they can create ceremonies to celebrate the water, plants, and animals that give-away. They may sprout seeds as we do in the winter cere-mony, in order to feel a relationship with plants as they awaken with life and grow. From our stories, they can learn to talk to the plants, showing the seedlings love and appreciation. They can also grow flowers in bowls within their lodges so they can expe-rience the joy of blooming.

They must try to eat natural foods, for their human-made foods will cause many dis-eases and rob them of their power. They should also exercise their muscles so that their bodies will remain alert and energetic. Most particularly, we should leave instructions for them to stay away from the object of moving pictures so it will not steal people's minds away from them. When people start to reconnect with their own personal power, each can begin the search for his or her purpose and path.

The pace of the future world will make it very difficult for people to discover which gifts they came to Earth to give-away. When they look into their hearts and see what brings the greatest joy, it will set them on a path toward that gift. The gift will need to be nurtured until it blooms into a radiant giveaway, and should be used to help the Earth and her many families of life in order to complete the circle. In this way, people can leave the world when they cross over knowing that they have helped create a better place.

Often, when we are in ceremony, hunting, or simply walking, we become calm and feel the connection with All That Is. Toward the end of the Fourth World, it will be challenging to experience this connectedness. Without tribal ceremonies or the opportunity to be close to the natural world, the future people will need to find a way to spend time in meditation. Even in the lodges of iron and mica, they can create a sacred space and sit calmly within it to quiet their minds. As they reach within themselves, they will create another path and connection with the All That Is, thus fulfilling a need that had remained empty for many years."

Chapter 13

The Birth of a New Beginning

Dream Catcher sat with her two children as they tried to grab polliwogs in the pond at Waterfall Meadow. Her mind drifted to the Dream Circle Council that would meet later that evening. Grandmother Crow had hinted that something special would take place this new moon.

It had been thirteen cycles of seasons since Grandmother had formed the council to share dreams. Since then, they had gathered together many prophecies of events that would come to pass for the Peaceful People and Mother Earth. Some of the dreams included in the songs-of-future-remembrance had even come from her own dream world.

She thought back over the past moon to see if any significant dreams had—"Mother, Mother! I caught one! I caught one!" Wind Eagle surprised her, bouncing up with his hands cupped together. "Can I take it home, Mother? I want to watch it grow into a frog. I will feed it and take care of it."

"Perhaps another time, Little Eagle. We will need to bring a large water gourd with us next time for it to live in. If you do not return it to the water soon, it will die. At this stage of its growth, the polliwogs can breathe only water, but as they grow and experience a life passage, they will begin to breathe air as we do."

Little Eagle returned to the pond and bent down to release the little wiggling being. "I want to see, Eagle!" Magpie ran over to the pond and craned her neck over Eagle, watching intently as he put his hands into the water to release the future frog. She leaned closer and closer, trying to see, until Eagle's hands suddenly shot out of the water and drenched her with a huge shower of polliwog and pond water. "Eagle!" she shrieked, indignant and laughing, and fought back with her own hand-fuls of water. Soon Dream Catcher had no choice but to join the water fight or get soaked, and shortly afterward, they all collapsed laughing on the grass.

Before the evening meeting, Grandmother Crow had asked Buffalo to bring her pipe to the Dream Circle. She opened the council with a dream.

"I have seen several generations of Peaceful People birthed before anyone in this circle was born except for my mate Painted Story. While watching over the tribe, Story and I have always worked to keep its medicine life active and focused on honoring the covenant with the Creator and Mother Earth. Before White Buffalo Woman invites us to pray with the sacred pipe, I would like to give a recent dream to the circle.

I awoke from sleep and left my lodge while it was still dark. I sat facing east, awaiting the twilight and the coming of sunrise, and in the silence, I thought of my first memory. I was looking into my mother's eyes, and suddenly a flood of memories showered me with my entire life.

As I reviewed my life, I realized that my spirit had come to Earth to form this Dream Circle. This council has been the most important and blissful part of my long life. While I saw my life's journey pass before me, twilight started glowing in the east.

Father Sun peeked over the distant mountain, and this morning he was a doorway to the World of Spirit. I stood and walked toward his door, bathed in a glowing light. My mother and father were there and they took me in their arms. I looked into my mother's eyes and felt the greatest peace I have ever felt since my first memory of life. Upon awakening, I realized that this dream had showed me my coming death.

When I pass on, White Buffalo Woman, my adopted daughter, will become the leader of this Dream Circle. When it is her time to join the World of Spirit, she will choose another, who I believe will be Dream Catcher.

This circle will continue down through the ages until the Fourth World comes to an end. I love and honor each of you for the time that we have shared together, especially Painted Story, who has been such a wonderful part of my soul's Earth Journey.

My daughter, you may begin your Sacred Pipe Ceremony now."

White Buffalo Woman called the Sacred Powers to the Dream Circle, then gave-away her prayers with the smoke in silence. The pipe was passed around the circle and each member also prayed in tearful quiet.

Grandfather Painted Story spoke into the stillness.

"I have always tried to accept life's abundance, both the blissful blessings and the contrary challenges. I cannot imagine walking the Earth without my wise, playful Crow. I will continue to give my dreams to this circle, although I feel my journey to the other side will follow close behind hers.

In my recent dream, time stretched out before me and I watched the Peaceful People for many, many cycles of seasons. Our tribe saw one prophecy after another come true. They realized that this was a medicine sign to stay on the path of the covenant, and so our tribe kept our ceremonies alive.

Keeping the covenant brought our tribe peace, joy, and prosperity for a very long time. Toward the end of the Fourth World, the Peaceful People were one of the few tribes who still walked in balance with the Earth and Sky, while the outside world continued in the path toward violence and destruction. After the gourd of ashes loosed its destruction for the first time, I saw that it was time to give-away our tribe's ancient wisdom. We must send an elder to the peace council in the House-of-Mica.

We will travel there four times, and if our message is not honored, we must prepare for the Purification of the Fourth

World. No matter what happens, we must continue reaching out with our wisdom to everyone who will listen. As long as there are people who follow the path of peace and have an appreciation for Earth's abundance, the fabric of the world will hold together. Although there will be changes if the fabric begins to tear, they will not cause the total destruction of our Mother Earth."

Grandmother reached out and took Painted Story's hand:

"The Great Day of Purification will be determined by how wide the inequity between the rich and the poor stretches. It will also depend on how the delicate Sacred Balance of Nature is honored by future humans.

In a recent dream, I saw Lying Down Mountain deep in snow with glaciers forming around all sides. Our songs of the future should include this warning: do not forget the power of the Land of Ice. If we begin to have late springs and early frosts, we must examine the Sacred Balance to see if it is being disturbed.

It is now time to close this dream council for tonight. Know that I love you all deeply and that I will continue to work toward peace and balance as I walk in the World of Spirit. Know that I will always be with you in spirit, and someday we may walk this Mother Earth together again."

Many cycles of the seasons later, Grandmother White Buffalo Woman held Magpie's new baby in her arms. Sweet Grass's little fingers grasped her long white braid, and she remembered holding Dream Catcher this way on their first trip to Waterfall Meadow. Her mind drifted back even further to how Grandmother Spider Woman held her when she was a baby.

The four priestesses enjoyed the spring day together. Magpie hugged Grandmother White Buffalo Woman close, and Dream Catcher looked into Sweet Grass's eyes. "I wish this day would never end."

Grandmother Buffalo smiled back. "With every beginning, there will always come an ending so that it may, in turn, birth a new beginning."

HO

Epilogue

I was born into a culture that, for me, had no functioning mythology. I have since wandered the Earth and searched through history and herstory to find myths to guide my life. Sitting in ceremony with tribal peoples in North America, Africa, Europe, Asia, and South America, I have tried to be open to the stories that felt good in my heart.

The stories of the Hopi people, who live in the heart of the country I was born into, have always resonated deep within me. I apologize if I have offended any of my Hopi elders by using many of their stories that I have been privileged to hear.

I wrote this story from my own imaginings of how life might have been thousands of years ago. The Hopi, whose name means Peaceful, still live in the oldest inhabited village in our country. I believe that their mythology is of great importance and may hold wisdom that can help our children's children continue to walk on this Mother Earth.

Many in-depth books have been written about The People and their prophecies. One of my mentors, Frank Waters, wrote *The Book of the Hopi*, which I often referred to when writing this story. I recommend it to all who would like a more comprehensive study of the Hopi People and their lives.

When I first started writing this book in the
winter of 2005, a message came to me from a friend
by e-mail. It helped me to write down the first
word, which is always the most difficult.

"You have been telling the people that
this is the Eleventh Hour. Now you must go
back and tell the people that this is the Hour.

And there are things to be considered:
Where are you living?
What are you doing?
What are your relationships?
Are you in right relation?
Where is your water?
Know your garden.
It is time to speak your Truth.
Create your community.
Be good to each other.
And do not look outside yourself for the leader.

This could be a good time!
There is a river flowing now very fast.
It is so great and swift that there are those
who will be afraid.
They will try to hold on to the shore.
They will feel they are being torn apart, and
they will suffer greatly.

Know the river has its destination.
The elders say we must let go of the shore,
push off into the middle of the river,
keep our eyes open,
and our heads above the water.
See who is in there with you and celebrate.

At this time in history, we are to take
nothing personally.
Least of all, ourselves.
For the moment that we do, our spiritual
growth and journey comes to a halt.
The time of the lone wolf is over.
Gather yourselves!

Banish the word struggle from your attitude
and your vocabulary.
All that we do now must be done in a
sacred manner and in celebration.

We are the ones we've been waiting for."

— *The Elders, Oraibi, Arizona, Hopi Nation*

The Wisdom of Chief Seattle

The spirit of White Buffalo Woman is returning at this time in history. During the last decade, several white buffalo calves have been born. To many Native Americans and other medicine people, this is a sign of great hope. It is a sign that the healing of Mother Earth has begun, bringing the unification of the black, red, white, and yellow races. On April 17, 2005, a white buffalo calf was born in British Columbia. The calf was named Spirit of Peace.

As the age of Pisces ends, we will experience the birth of a new age, Aquarius, the time of a new beginning. Ancient myths may help us through this transition. We must now build more functioning myths into our culture, and America's indigenous people give us powerful roots from which our vision can grow. I feel that our new myths should include seeing the Earth as sacred, as our ancient teachers have taught us. This teaching is powerfully expressed by the words of Chief Seattle in answer to President Pierce's offer on behalf of the United States to buy the tribal land of the Northwest Elder's people:

"How can you buy or sell the sky? The land? The idea is strange to us. If we do not own the freshness of the air and the sparkle of the water, how can you buy them? Every part of this Earth is sacred to my people. Every shining pine needle, every sandy shore, every mist in the dark woods, every meadow, every humming insect. All are holy in the memory and experience of my people.

If we sell you our land, remember that the air is precious to us and shares its spirit with all the life it supports. The wind that gave our grandfather his first breath also received his last sigh. The wind also gives our children the spirit of life. So if we sell you our land, you must keep it apart and sacred, a place where man can go to taste the wind that is sweetened by the meadow flowers.

Will you teach your children what we have taught our children? That the Earth is our Mother? What befalls the Earth befalls all the sons of the Earth.

This we know: The Earth does not belong to man, but man belongs to the Earth. All things are connected like the blood that unites us all. Man did not weave the web of life; he is merely a strand in it. Whatever he does to the web, he does to himself.

We are part of the Earth and She is part of us. The perfumed flowers are our sisters.

The bear, the deer, the great eagle, these are our brothers. The rivers are our brothers. They carry our canoes and feed our children.

Each ghostly reflection in the clear water of the lakes tells of events in the memories of my people. The water's murmurs are the voice of my father's father.

We love this Earth as a newborn loves its mother's heartbeat. So if we sell you our land, love it as we have loved it. Care for it as we have cared for it. Hold in your mind a memory of the land, as it is when you receive it. Preserve the land for all children and love it as God loves us all.

One thing we know: There is only one God. No man, be he red or white, can be apart. We are brothers after all."

List of Illustrations

I have included the pictures of my artwork in *Lying Down Mountain* so that the reader can feel the wisdom of the archetypal mythology through images as well as words. These symbols speak not only to our minds, but to a deeper part of us. They speak to us as our dreams speak.

Good Medicine, Heyoka

Page viii

"**Earth Mother.**" White Buffalo Woman is the Native American archetype for the Earth Mother, and she is depicted here blessing the world of Sky Father's spirits with the ceremonial pipe. As she prays over the shield of spirit, the animals awaken with physical life. The world is now both spirit and substance animated with the breath of life.

Page x

"**Sky Father.**" The eagle symbolizes First Spirit, called Sky Father by the Native Americans. Within Native American culture, birds are depicted as spirit, and the bird-human portrayed in this sculpture represents an archetypal image that appears throughout many different cultures. As Sky Father touches the shield of life, his single spirit becomes many spirits.

171

Page xii

"Jaguar Priestess." (front). The Mayans believed that the jaguar can be seen dancing around the North Star in the constellation of the Big Dipper, with a long curving tail and spotted with stars. The jaguar keeps the balance of memories past, present, and future.

Page xii

"Rain Bird Shield." (back). Rain Bird Shield is a Hopi symbol of the creative spiral, one of the world's oldest and most sacred symbols. It is the spiral movement of creation that incorporates all elements that bring forth life.

Page 10

"Buffalo Shield." When a herd of buffalo is attacked by predators, the adults form a protective circle around the young calves. When the Native Americans saw this, they called the buffalos "the keepers of the circle." They knew that everything has a place on the medicine wheel of the Universe, and within this one great circle, there are many wheels that help us to understand life.

Page 22

"Sacred Twins." Tezcatlipoca is the jaguar deity, the smoking mirror, the keeper of the night sky, and the master of astronomy. Quetzalcoatl is the plumed serpent, keeper of the day sky, and the fire-bringer. Together, the two Mayan deities kindled the first fire of creation. The forked Sundance Tree of Life between the twins again refers to the Sacred Balance and the duality of life.

Page 40

"Spirit Elk." To the Native Americans, the eagle is the symbol of spirit and the messenger of the sky. Flying higher than any other creature, eagles are also known to possess the keenest sight among all animals. The medicine power of the elk is stamina, strength, and comradeship.

Page 52

"Warriors of the Rainbow." According to the ancient prophecies of the Native Americans, the spirit of their peoples will be born anew into all of the races that have gathered in our land, and each of the different races of rainbow colors will see that we are all one family.

Page 66

"White Buffalo Woman Shrine." Long ago, two men crossing the plains of America saw a beautiful woman dressed in white buckskin approaching. She came holding a pipe in her hands and taught the men to honor everything in the Universe while putting tobacco in the pipe. The pipe was to be an altar and the center of their ceremonies. As the woman walked away, she turned into a white buffalo.

Page 78

"Spider Woman." To the Pueblo Indians, Spider Woman is the Creator of the Universe. She began by spinning two threads: east to west and north to south. She made the people from yellow, red, black, and white clay and also produced two daughters who created the sun and the moon.

Page 88

"Crow Mother."

Rhea Kronia, Mother Crow
 Holding together time and space
Wisdom Woman, nurturing Earth
 Giving teacher, Grandmother Crone
Angwusnasomtaka, Crow Mother
 Kachina of initiation
Singing Valkrie, angels flying
 Bring our souls to spirit realms
Sacred Crow, eldest ancestor
 Watching generations come and go

Page 102

"Diana (The Huntress)." The Queen of Heaven and Sacred Huntress is called Artemis by the Grecians and Diana by the Romans. She is the Triple Goddess: Lunar Virgin, Mother of all Creatures, and the Huntress or Destroyer. She retains her rightful role as the Great Goddess, embodiment of strength and power: swift, straight, and deadly as her arrows.

Page 120

"Flying Dreams." Some of the first writing we possess from ancient cultures speaks about dream interpretation. Our ancestors placed great importance on the symbols that appear in our dreams, as have modern psychologists. In many cultures, flying is a symbol of spirit, and it may be especially helpful to explore the meaning of our dream world when we have flying dreams.

Page 132

"Grandmother North Making Snow." Grandmother North gives us a strong helping hand as she holds us in the cold grip of winter. Her cold helps control the insects that kill trees, and although her touch often seems harsh, the beauty of Grandmother North and her snow hold wisdom and balance.

Page 144

"Dryad (Nature Spirit)." Many people believe that in Nature, each tree, plant, and flower has a spirit living within it. This spirit is the consciousness that sleeps within the seed and guides the growth of the plant throughout its life. Tree spirits are also called Dryads.

Page 154

"**Birth of an Age.**" The myth of the Phoenix says that at the beginning of a New Age, the phoenix hatches from an egg within a fiery nest. The two phoenix birds on either side of the burning nest are the New Age and its mirror, the former age. The burning nest symbolizes the passing of the old way and the birth of the new way.

Page 162

"**Earth Father.**" In the southwest plains of America, the name for Earth Father is Thundering Earth, and he represents the archetypal Horned God found in the mythology of many cultures. The Horned God dances a circle of protection around Earth Mother, the Creatress. Without him to guard her, the Earth Mother would not have a protected place in which to work her magic of birthing.

Page 170

"**Sky Mother.**" Sky Mother is the Sacred Void that existed before the manifest universe. She is the Sacred Womb of creation, the darkness out of which light was born. The lightning bolts are the First Spirit (Sky Father) flashing through the blackness of the Sacred Void.

Page 179

"Sweet Medicine." The Forest Father, called Sweet Medicine by one of the northern Native American tribes, believed that every part of creation has a lesson to teach. Only when our minds become silent can we hear the language spoken by Mother Earth. Each encounter with an animal can become an oracle, giving special meaning to the moment, especially if the meeting occurs in a sacred space like the Sundance or a vision quest.

Page 180

"Shaman." The first man on Earth was also the first shaman. He taught that all animals were related to our human family. Every encounter with an animal was a gift from the animal powers. In mythical symbolism, the shaman is like the Horned God or Father Earth that is found in cultures all over the world.

EPILOGUE

Page 166

"Miracle." The white buffalo calf, by Keith Powell
www.powellartstudio.com

"Crow Mother." Cover art is by Willow LaLand
www.willowlaland.com

To view more of Heyoka Merrifield's artwork,
visit his website at www.heyoka-art.com.

Printed in the United States
By Bookmasters